Six Who Ran

KENDELL FOSTER CROSSEN
Writing as
M.E. CHABER

STEEGER BOOKS / **2020**

PUBLISHED BY STEEGER BOOKS
Visit steegerbooks.com for more books like this.

PUBLISHING HISTORY

Hardcover
New York: Holt, Rinehart & Winston (A Rinehart Suspense Novel), July 1964.
Toronto: Holt, Rinehart & Winston of Canada, 1964.
Roslyn, NY: Detective Book Club #272, Walter J. Black, Inc., 1964. (With *The Laughter Trap* by Judson Philips and *The Departure of Mr. Gaudette* by Doris Miles Disney.)
London: T. V. Boardman (American Bloodhound Mystery #498), 1965.

Paperback
New York: Paperback Library (63-380), A Milo March Mystery, #10, July 1970. Cover by Robert McGinnis.

ISBN: 978-1-61827-534-9

Milo March is a hard-drinking, womanizing, wisecracking, James-Bondian character. He always comes out on top through a combination of personality, bluff, bravado, luck, skill, experience, and intellect. He is a shrewd judge of human character, a crack shot, and a deeper character than I have found in most of the other spy/thriller novels I've read. But, above all, he is a con-man—and a very good one. It is Milo March himself who makes the series worth reading.

—Don Miller, *The Mystery Nook* fanzine 12

Steeger Books is proud to reissue twenty-three vintage novels and stories by M.E. Chaber, whose Milo March Mysteries deliver mile-a-minute action and breezily readable entertainment for thriller buffs.

Milo is an Insurance Investigator who takes on the tough cases. Organized crime, grand theft, arson, suspicious disappearances, murders, and millions and millions of dollars—whatever it is, Milo is just the man for the job. Or even the only man for it.

During World War II, Milo was assigned to the OSS and later the CIA. Now in the Army Reserves, with the rank of Major, he is recalled for special jobs behind the Iron Curtain. As an agent, he chops necks, trusses men like chickens to steal their uniforms, shoots point blank at secret police—yet shows compassion to an agent from the other side.

Whatever Milo does, he knows how to do it right. When the work is completed, he returns to his favorite things: women, booze, and good food, more or less in that order....

THE MILO MARCH MYSTERIES

As another scribe once said:

It seems she hangs upon the cheek of night
As a rich jewel in an Ethiop's ear;
Beauty too rich for use, for earth too dear!

CONTENTS

BEFORE

Storm King Mountain reared in all its grandeur above Newburgh, Cornwall, Highland Falls, even the majesty of the Hudson River, and finally above West Point, until its peaks flirted with the clouds that came down for a closer look.

The armored truck, looking like a small replica of the mountain's strength, left Highland Falls and started over the mountain for Newburgh and its next stop.

It had barely started up the mountain when a state highway truck pulled up. Two men got out, lifted a heavy sign from the rear of the truck, and placed it in the center of the road. The sign announced *Road Closed for Construction.* The men trudged back to the truck and returned with a smaller sign, which they placed beside the road. This one simply said *Detour.* An arrow pointed to an alternate route. The men went back to the truck and drove away.

The armored truck passed the West Point gate and wound up into the mountain. It rounded a hairpin turn, and the driver braked. There was a State Police car parked across the road, its red light blinking. A state trooper walked over to the armored truck, flashlight in hand. He waited patiently until the driver opened his door.

"What's wrong, officer?" the driver asked.

"A bad accident just around the curve," the officer said

crisply. "My partner is there and we've already phoned for an ambulance, but we need some help before it gets here. Can you give us a hand?"

"I guess so," the driver said. He looked at the man beside him. "Let's go, Jim. Lock up."

The state trooper waited patiently while the two men got out of the truck and locked the doors. When they turned to face him, he had his gun out. He shot them both before they even had time to show surprise. As they fell to the ground, the door of the police car opened and another man got out.

"Hurry up," the man in the trooper's uniform said. He bent down and took a ring of keys from the dead driver.

They dragged the two dead men over to the police car and loaded them in the rear seat. They took a suitcase out of the car and opened it. From it, they pulled two uniforms exactly like the ones worn by the dead men. They changed quickly, putting their other clothes into the suitcase and tossing it into the armored truck. Then they started the motor of the police car, put it in drive gear, and watched as it rolled over the side of the mountain. It was a long time before they heard the final crash from below.

They walked back to the armored truck and climbed in. They drove for about a mile and then turned off on a weed-infested road that had been the original path over the mountain. They drove slowly over the old road for about four miles. Then the headlights picked out two cars parked among the trees, beside the road. The armored truck stopped in front of them and its lights went off.

The two men got out of the truck and opened its rear door.

They were joined by two figures from the parked car. The four of them quickly and quietly took the bags from the truck and loaded them into the two passenger cars. They drove away, leaving the truck behind.

When they reached 9 W, they followed it to Route 32, then turned south. They reached Mountainville and took Taylor Road. They followed the winding road until they reached the top of the hill. There were no houses near, but there were two cars parked with their lights out. The approaching cars blinked their lights and were answered by the lights of the parked vehicles.

The two approaching cars parked behind the others. Once more the bags were shifted, but this time there were six people to do the work, so it took even less time. When they were finished, they took rags and carefully went over the doors, the steering wheels, and the instrument panels of the cars they had driven to this place. When they had done this to their satisfaction, they closed the doors, being careful not to leave fresh fingerprints. They got into the other cars, three to each one, and drove off.

The whole thing had taken less than an hour. ...

ONE

March. Milo March. That's me. At least, that's what it says on the door of my office on Madison Avenue in New York City, and nobody's given me an argument about it since it was put there. The rest of the legend on the door says that I'm an insurance investigator. My license says that I'm a private investigator. So does my gun permit. I guess they're all correct.

It was a quiet morning. I had the morning *Times* and a container of coffee. My feet were on the desk and all was right with my world at the moment. Then the telephone rang. I let the paper drop to my lap and picked up the receiver.

"Hello," I said.

"Milo, boy, how are you?" a hearty voice asked. I recognized it at once. It belonged to Martin Raymond, a vice-president at Intercontinental Insurance. It probably meant a job, so I was respectful, but not too much so.

"I'm not sure yet," I said. "It's only my second cup of coffee."

"Coffee?" he said mockingly. "I thought you always started the day with a dry martini."

"Only when I'm on an expense account," I said evenly. "This is my own money I'm spending now."

"Good."

"What's good about it?"

He chuckled. "It means that you're not too busy at the moment, and I think I have a job for you."

"You think?" I said. "Call me back when you're sure."

"Wait a minute," he said. "Can you run over here for a minute?"

"No," I said. "I might walk over, or take a cab, but I'm getting too old to run."

"Maybe I should look for someone younger," he said, and I could tell he thought he'd scored a big joke, "but come over as soon as you can." He hung up.

I finished my coffee and threw the container in the wastebasket. I went out and took a taxi up Madison Avenue. If he had a job for me, there was no reason to walk.

Intercontinental Insurance has its own office on Madison Avenue, one of those new peekaboo buildings made of glass and concrete. I rode up to the fifteenth floor, where all the executives were caged. The reception room was a good clue to where their money went. The carpeting on the floor, the modern art on the walls, the modernistic furniture, were all as lush as they could be, but they faded into nothing when the receptionist was sighted. She was a beautiful redhead with measurements that would have made Anita Ekberg look like an underfed orphan.

She recognized me, but didn't let on. "Yes?" she said.

"I'm glad you said that," I told her solemnly. "I've been waiting for months for you to say that one word."

She gave me the benefit of a small smile. "Do you want to see Mr. Raymond?"

I sighed. "I don't want to, but I guess he's about all I will see."

That wasn't really quite accurate, for there was a beautiful view as she leaned over the telephone. She announced that I was there, waited a minute, then replaced the phone.

She looked up at me. "You may go in, Mr. March," she said.

"Fine," I said. I looked down at her. "Take a deep breath."

Without thinking, she obeyed.

"Beautiful," I murmured.

She got it then. She exhaled, her face taking on a touch of pink. "What was the idea of that?"

"Blame it on Vic Tanny,"* I said gravely. "He wants all of us to stay fit."

I left before she could think of an answer. I walked down the long corridor and turned in at Raymond's office. His secretary greeted me with a smile and motioned for me to go on in. I opened the door to the private office and stepped inside.

It was a nice office, furnished with antiques, including a cobbler's bench and an old cupboard that had been converted into a bar. The original owners must have been turning over in their graves.

"Hi, Milo," he said, looking up. "Glad you were able to get here."

"It was tough," I said, dropping into the chair beside his desk. I lit a cigarette. "Madison Avenue was covered with slogans, and I didn't think we'd get through."

"That's my boy," he said, "anything for a laugh."

---

* Vic Tanny was a pioneer in creating the modern health club. (All footnotes were added by the editor.)

Martin Raymond was a great one for remarks like that.

"Are you free for a job?" he asked.

"I can take a job, but I'm not free."

He sighed. "When were you ever. This is a tough one, Milo."

"When did you ever give me any other kind? What's the case?"

"A week ago," he said, "an armored truck was picking up money from banks to be delivered to the Federal Reserve. In Upstate New York. The truck made a pickup in Highland Falls and started over the mountain for Newburgh. It never got there."

"A heist?"

He nodded. "The two guards were found three days later, over the side of the mountain. Both had been shot, placed in a car disguised as a state police car, and run off the road. The armored truck was found on an old road that hasn't been used in years, leading down from the mountain. There was no money in it. No fingerprints either. State highway signs had been placed at both ends of the regular road over the mountain, so that no one would come along and interrupt the thieves. It had been well planned."

"How much did they get?"

He sighed again. "One million dollars in cash. No records on the bills. Plus about a half million in securities and bonds. Those will be more difficult to get rid of."

"Clues?"

"None."

"Sounds like a juicy one. You carried the insurance on it?"

"On all of it, cash and securities and bonds."

"Do you have any more information?"

He shook his head. "That's it. Oh, I can give you the name of the man in charge of the investigation for the State Police. He's Lieutenant Paul Haynes. You can have the file if you like, but there's nothing else in it."

"It sounds like the kind of case that you always give me," I said. "A hundred a day and expenses?"

He nodded. "And a bonus if you succeed. I think I can promise you it'll be a big one."

"Depending on how much money I recover," I said ironically. "Okay, Martin, I'll take it. When do you want me to start?"

"As soon as you can." He looked as if he were suffering pain. "I suppose you want some expense money?"

"Naturally," I said cheerfully. "You don't expect me to spend my own money, do you?"

"How much?"

"We'd better start with about two thousand."

He winced.

"You know damn well, Martin, that this is not going to be a short case. Anybody smart enough to walk away from a job like that without leaving any clues is not going to be found in a day or two. So you better plan on the two thousand just being the first installment on expenses." He knew that I was right, but it didn't make him look any happier.

"All right," he said. "See my secretary and she'll give you the authorization. Keep in touch."

"Sure. I'll be in touch as soon as I need more expense money."

I gave him my best smile and left. I stopped beside his secretary's desk. She looked up.

"I can see the triumph in your eyes," she said. "You made him part with some more money."

"Two thousand dollars," I said. "A man needs cigarette money and carfare."

"What kind of car? A Rolls-Royce?" She scribbled on a memo and handed it to me. "You know the way to the cashier? You ought to. You've been there more often than anyone in the company."

"I always speak well of you," I said, taking the slip. "Besides, I'll take you to the best lunch in town as soon as I come back."

"Promise her anything, but give her a hotdog," she said.

"You have no gratitude, woman," I said stiffly. "I give my all for dear old Continental and all I get are insults. Oh, well ..."

She laughed. "Milo, you're a con man. Run along and get your loot. I'll be busy. Every time you take a case for us, Mr. Raymond is a nervous wreck until the case is over and the expense vouchers have been filed away."

"It's good for him," I told her. "It's the only excitement he ever gets. I'll see you, honey."

I went down the corridor to the cashier's office and presented the memo. In return, I received a pack of nice, crisp money, which I put in my pocket.

I went back to my office and left word with my answering service that I would be out of town for an indefinite period. Then I took a cab down to my apartment on Perry Street. I packed a bag and took another cab to a car rental agency. A few minutes of time and a few dollars, and they put me in the driver's seat. I drove up the West Side Highway, crossed the George Washington Bridge, and turned right on the Palisades Parkway. I knew the way, for I had worked on a case only a few months earlier that had terminated in that same area.*

The drive took about an hour and a half. When I reached Cornwall, I stayed on 9-W toward Newburgh. I stopped at the first likely motel, registered, and left my bag. Then I drove on to the nearest restaurant. It was already noon. I went in and had a couple of martinis and some lunch. Then I drove to the State Police barracks. There was a sergeant on duty at the desk.

"Lieutenant Paul Haynes," I said.

"Who wants to see him?"

"I do."

He didn't like that. "Who are you?"

"Milo March."

"Why do you want to see the Lieutenant?"

"About a case he's working on."

"What case?"

I smiled. "I'll discuss it with him, if you don't mind."

"We'll see," he said darkly. He picked up the phone and pressed a buzzer.

"There's a man who says his name is Milo March and he wants to talk to you about a case you're working on. He won't say what the case is." He listened for a minute, then hung up. He looked at me. "He'll see you. Second door down the hall."

I nodded and walked down the corridor. I reached the

* See *Uneasy Lies the Dead* by M.E. Chaber.

second door and opened it. The Lieutenant was a pleasant-looking young man, his appearance similar to all other state policemen. It was probably the uniform.

"March?" he asked.

I nodded and stepped inside, closing the door behind me.

"Insurance dick," he said, as though he had a file on me inside his head. "You were up here on a case about a year ago. Lieutenant Pilus didn't think you were very cooperative."

"I'm flattered," I told him.

He gave me a mechanical smile. "It's my job to know what goes through here. What do you want this time, March?"

"The armored truck job. I understand that you're in charge of it."

He nodded. "What's your interest in it?"

"I work for Intercontinental Insurance. They carried the policies on the entire million and a half."

"That's a nice sum of money. I gather that your company doesn't believe the New York State Police can solve the crime?"

"Not at all," I said. "We may have some slight suspicion that the case has moved outside of your jurisdiction."

"There are other state police and city police, all of them quite competent."

I sighed. "I'm aware of that, Lieutenant, having worked with most of them at one time or another. Intercontinental Insurance is not worrying about whether the police are competent or not. They are worried about their money—a million and a half dollars. It's a habit they have. And sometimes I can work on a case and not have to worry about crossing state lines—or even national borders. And I always cooperate with the local police, no matter where I am."

"That wasn't the impression I had from the report on your last visit."

I lit a cigarette and looked at him. "I didn't write the report. I brought in two wanted men. When one of them was on the point of killing me, I could hardly ask his permission to call Lieutenant Pilus. And if you'll check the newspaper stories, you'll find there is no mention of anyone named March and there are quite a few of the good lieutenant. What the hell am I supposed to do? Hold his hand, too?"

He laughed. "Well, one thing in the report was right. It said you operated on a short fuse. What do you want to know, March?"

"I'd like to know what you've found out so far."

"Not much," he admitted. "We believe that six people were involved. Three passenger cars were stolen within a period of five days before the robbery. One of them was converted into a State Police car with the aid of a blinker light stolen from a police car in a town about fifteen miles north of here. There's an empty warehouse on Route 32 which was used for converting the car. The other two stolen cars were found the morning after the robbery on a back road between Mountainville and Washingtonville. No prints or anything else in any of the three cars. Nothing on the armored car either. The two guards were both shot with a .38, but we haven't found the gun. There was one light truck stolen from the State Highway Department the afternoon of the robbery, and it was abandoned as soon as it had served its purpose. No prints on that either."

"Any leads on the six?"

He shook his head. "Not yet. But we haven't had much time. We'll dig up something."

"What have you been doing on that?"

"So far as we know, the guards are the only ones who saw the robbers—and they're both dead. Obviously the men were not from around here, so we've been checking hotels and motels. So far we have a list of about fifty names that fit the time schedule. It'll take a little while to check them all out."

"Why obvious that they're not from here?"

"The only big criminals we have are bookies. This job was too big for the local talent."

"I'm inclined to agree," I said, "but I just wanted to hear your reasoning. Is that all?"

"That's about it."

"May I see the reports?"

He shook his head. "Sorry. It's against regulations."

"I'm an old hand at running up against regulations," I said with a sigh. "Well, there's nothing to do but go to work. Thanks, Lieutenant."

"You'll still cooperate?" he asked.

"Sure," I said. "If the case is still in your jurisdiction, I'll cooperate. If not, I may save it for some other cop. I'll see you around."

"Yes," he said. He was watching me thoughtfully as I left.

I drove back to my motel. I took off my coat and stretched out on the bed. Finally, I faced the fact that I was wasting my time. There was no way except through drudgery. I got out a classified phone book from the cabinet next to the bed and started leafing through it. I had already decided to ignore the hotels. Motels felt like a better bet, and I didn't have as much time as the State Police.

After about an hour I had a list, grouped according to location. I sighed and put on my coat. Then I started with the motel I was in. From there I went to one after another, slowly collecting names, addresses, and license numbers—all of people who had checked in a week to ten days before the robbery and had checked out the day of the robbery or the following day. The list had thirty-eight names on it. But there wasn't any record of six people checking in together.

It was already evening when I finished. I drove back to Cornwall and found a restaurant. I had a couple of martinis and then ordered dinner.

When I'd finished dinner, I went out and bought a bottle of V.O. at the nearest liquor store. Then I drove back to the motel. I fixed a drink, took off enough clothes to be comfortable, and started going over the list. I didn't know what I was looking for; I was just hoping I'd stumble onto something.

I was going through the list for the fourth time, and about to give up, when I finally noticed something. It wasn't much. There were three license numbers from three different motels that had the same letters before the numbers. This was not so much by itself, for there were other matching letters on the list, but it suddenly struck me that there was something familiar about these particular license plates. I thought about it a minute, then put on my shirt and went outside.

I'd been right. The letters on the three license plates were the same as the ones on the plates of my rented car. I went back to my motel room feeling the first twinge of excitement.

TWO

The next morning, after a good night's sleep, I checked out of the motel and headed back for New York City. An hour and a half later I was there. I went directly to the car rental agency. I showed the manager the three license numbers and waited while he went through his records. Finally, he looked up and nodded.

"Those were our cars," he said. "All three cars went out eighteen days ago and were returned eight days ago. I didn't notice it before, but I see that the mileage was pretty much the same on all three cars. The lowest mileage was two hundred and fifty miles and the highest was three hundred and fifty."

"All three taken out together?"

"No. One was taken out in the morning, one about noon, and the other in the afternoon. They were returned the same day, but not at the same time."

"Who took them out?"

He glanced at the records. "Peter Jackson, Edward Myers, and Joseph Sforza."

Those weren't the names from the motels, but that didn't mean anything.

"The names checked with their driving licenses?"

"Of course. I don't let any cars go out without that kind of check. You know that."

I did. The names he had were probably the right ones. "Addresses?" I asked.

He nodded. "I'll write them down for you. They're all three different." He pulled off a sheet from a memo pad and wrote on it. He pushed it across to me.

"Anything else, Milo?" he asked.

"I guess not, Paul," I said. "It would help if you could tell me where they are now, but you can't. It's a sure bet they're not at these addresses."

"Are we going to have trouble over this?" he asked quietly.

"I don't think so. I'll keep you out of it if I can."

"Thanks," he said. "You want to turn your car in?"

"Not yet. I may need it for another day or two. I'll see you."

I took the slip of paper and left. I drove down to the Village and found a place to park not far from my apartment on Perry Street. I took my baggage up to the apartment, picked up my mail, and read it. There was nothing of any importance. Then I looked at the memo slip. Peter Jackson's address was Barrow Street—about three blocks from me. Joseph Sforza lived on East Third Street. Edward Myers lived on West End Avenue.

I thought I knew the first answers, but I had to start sometime. I went out and walked over to Barrow Street. There was no Jackson listed on the mailboxes. I rang the superintendent's bell. After a couple of minutes, the door opened and an old man looked out at me.

"I'm looking for a Peter Jackson," I said.

"They moved out," he said. "About three weeks ago."

"They?"

"Him and his wife. At least, she was supposed to be his wife. That's what they said when they moved in."

"How long did they live here?"

"You a cop?" he wanted to know.

"No. Insurance company. It's about his policy. If he doesn't get in touch with us, or we don't find out where he is, it may be canceled."

He nodded slowly. "They was here about two years."

"What was his job?"

"Don't you know?"

"I only know what he was doing when he took out the policy. That was several years ago. I just thought that I might find him through his company."

"I ain't sure," he said. "He did something for one of the theaters around here, I think."

"You don't know which one?"

"No."

"Did his wife work?"

"I don't think so. She was always around whenever I had to go to the apartment."

"What was her name?"

"Betty. At least, that was the name on the mailbox." He hesitated a minute. "She also used the last name of Bell for mail. Maybe they wasn't married."

"Maybe," I said with a shrug. "Do you know where they moved?"

"No. Folks don't usually tell me. I guess they tell the post office, but not me."

"Okay," I said. "What kind of tenants were they?"

"Like all tenants," he said. He sounded tired. "Sometimes they fought; sometimes they had parties; sometimes they didn't do anything. They're all the same—except the ones who are different."

"I guess so," I said. "Thanks."

I left and went up to Seventh Avenue. There were a couple of off-Broadway theaters there, but neither one of them was open. I went and got the car and drove crosstown to East Third Street. It was a battered old building. There was no Joseph Sforza on the mailboxes. It took me a little longer to find the superintendent here, but I finally located him in a candy store across the street—not that it did me any good. Sforza had lived there alone for a year, and had moved away three weeks before. No forwarding address. No information about where he had worked or where he had lived before. He'd paid his rent and behaved himself, and that was all.

I drove uptown to West End Avenue and 80th Street. The address was a small brownstone apartment house. The information was about the same. Edward Myers had lived there for one year and six months—alone. He was a nice, quiet tenant. He'd had a lease, but had found someone who was willing to take it over when he'd decided to move three weeks earlier. He'd told the superintendent that he had a new job in Florida, and that was why he was leaving. There was no forwarding address. No one knew where he had worked while he was living at the West End Avenue address.

I drove back downtown and parked the car. I went over to Jack Delaney's and had a drink and some lunch. Then I walked around the corner and stopped at the first theater. It was called the Actor's Globe. I stepped inside. There was a pretty blonde behind a table waiting for people to come in and buy tickets.

"Yes?" she said, before I was all the way in.

"I'd like to talk to someone in charge," I said.

She looked disappointed, but she picked up the phone and pressed a button.

"Scotti," she said, "there's a man here who wants to talk to you." She hung up and looked at me. "Just a minute," she told me.

I nodded and retreated to the wall. Two people came in and bought tickets.

Finally, a woman came up the steps from somewhere below and glanced at me. She was maybe in her early thirties, not pretty, but with a wise look in her eyes. By wise, I don't mean wisdom. It was the kind of wise look that's supposed to tell everyone that she knows the score even if she doesn't know what game is being played.

"I'm Scotti Poulson," she said. "You wanted to see me?"

"If you're part of the management, I do."

"I'm one of the owners. What is it?"

I took out my wallet and showed her my identification card from Intercontinental. "I'm from the insurance company," I said. "It's about someone who presumably worked here."

"Who?" Her voice was like crisp lettuce.

"Peter Jackson."

She laughed. "I suppose you could say he worked here. He helped out with the lights and scenery for maybe three months."

"Did he make a good salary?"

She laughed again. "What do you mean? He didn't get a salary, except when there was a show running. So he was paid for three weeks, I think, before we let him go."

"When was that?"

"About four weeks ago."

"Why did you let him go?"

"He ordered some costumes from Monig Theatrical Costumes and had them delivered here. He didn't charge them to us, I'll say that much for him, but we figured he was planning on giving us some competition, so we let him go so he'd have plenty of time to work at it."

"And did he?"

"Did he what?"

"Start giving you any competition?"

"Not that I know of. Maybe he couldn't raise the money, or maybe he ordered the costumes because he only liked to dress in drag."

"Could be," I said. "Know where he lives?"

"Barrow Street. I can give you the address and his phone number if you like."

"He's already left there," I told her. "Thank you very much." I left quickly.

It was still early in the afternoon. I started for the car, then changed my mind and took a cab. We went up to 47th Street and I found Monig Theatrical Costumes. I went in and asked for the manager. He finally came out—a wispy little man.

"Yes, yes?" he asked, as though I had already wasted half his day.

"I'd like some information."

"What show are you with?"

"My own," I said. I showed him my Intercontinental card.

"Insurance? We already have all the insurance we want."

"I'm not selling any," I said. "And I still want some information."

"Our only business is the rental of costumes. So do you want information about costs and our variety? We have anything you can possibly want, and the prices are the lowest in the world."

"How about a full-size dinosaur costume?" I asked gravely.

He gave me a scornful look. "I don't have any time for jokes."

"Then why don't you let me tell you what I want, instead of trying to second-guess me? About three weeks ago you rented some costumes to a Peter Jackson. The address was Actor's Globe theater in the Village. I'd like some information about the transaction."

"Why should I give it to you? You're not from the police."

I was getting a little tired of him. "Because," I said evenly, "if you don't, the cops will be here, and I don't think you'll be so coy. It's easier with me."

He grunted, but he turned away and took his books from the side of the cash register. "Three weeks ago?" he asked.

"Approximately."

He leafed through the pages and finally stopped. "We rented some costumes to a Peter Jackson three weeks ago. He paid in advance and we delivered the costumes to him at Actor's Globe theater. He returned the costumes a week ago."

"Did he return them or did you pick them up?"

"He returned them."

"What were the costumes?"

"Two state police uniforms and two guard uniforms."

"Do you know what he used them for?"

"No. We don't ask questions like that."

"Did you have any address for him except the theater?"

"No."

"Have the costumes been rented since then?"

"No." He looked at me with a slight smile on his face. "But that won't do you any good."

"What do you mean?"

"They've been cleaned."

"I'm glad to hear you're so hygienic," I said dryly. "Was he alone when he came in to rent the costumes?"

"The records wouldn't show that, but I think he was."

"Okay," I said. "Thanks for everything. You've been peachy."

I turned and left. I went straight back to my apartment. When I got there I picked up the phone and called Lieutenant Johnny Rockland at police headquarters. I was lucky. He was in.

"Hi, Milo," he said. "What do you want this time?"

"Who said I wanted anything?"

"I did. It's the only time you call me. You're not like other citizens. You don't call to report crimes. You call to pick my brains so you can make the cops look like chumps."

"Far be it from me to try to improve on the Lord's work," I said solemnly.

"Very funny," he said bitingly. "Do you want something or did you just feel like wasting the taxpayers' money?"

"Okay, Johnny," I said. "I want to ask you what you know about three men."

"Who?"

"Peter Jackson, Joseph Sforza, and Eddie Myers."

"Are you looking for them?"

"Yes."

"I can tell you where to find one of them—Eddie Myers."

"Where?"

"In the city morgue. They pulled him out of the East River two days ago. There were three .38 bullets in him. He'd been in the river for about three days."

"Who killed him?"

"We don't know. Myers was on parole from Sing Sing. He was being watched fairly closely because he'd been associating with known criminals. We haven't been able to find any of them for questioning."

"I don't suppose the known criminals would be the other two men I asked about?"

"You win the kewpie doll," he said. "For several weeks he's been seen in the company of Peter Jackson and Joseph Sforza—and two other men, George Dallin and Tony Petrie. All of them have records."

"What kind of records?"

"Robbery and armed robbery. Jackson was also tried on one count of manslaughter and one of first-degree murder. He beat both of those raps."

"Know anything about a girl named Betty Bell?"

"Sure. Jackson's girlfriend. She served a sentence for shop-lifting about four years ago."

"Any idea where they are now?"

"Not the slightest," he said cheerfully. "They all disap-peared from their usual haunts about three weeks ago. Myers, too. We've had no lead on any of them until Myers was fished out of the river. We've got bulletins out on the others, but no word yet. Why are you interested in them, Milo?"

"I think they're the ones who pulled that armored truck job upstate."

He whistled softly. "Got anything to go on?"

"Yes. Jackson worked with an off-Broadway theater. Three weeks ago Jackson rented some costumes from Monig Theat-rical Costumes. What he rented was State Police uniforms and guard uniforms—like those used on the job. The costumes were returned a week ago."

"You may have something," he said. "Anything else?"

"That's all at the moment. I'll keep in touch."

"Do that," he said, and hung up.

I stayed in the apartment for a while, thinking about the case. Not that it did me any good. I simply didn't have anything else, and had no idea where to start. Finally I left, walking down to Sheridan Square, where I bought an evening paper. Then I went down Commerce Street to the Blue Mill. I sat at the end of the bar and ordered a martini. I opened the newspaper and read while I sipped the drink.

I was already on my second martini when I saw an item that brought me up short. It was a small piece, datelined from upstate. It said that an unidentified man's body had been pulled from the Hudson River. He'd been shot and had been dead for about a week.

I went to the phone booth and called Johnny Rockland. He'd already left the office, so I called him at home. He didn't sound too happy when he came to the phone.

"I know you promised to keep in touch," he said sourly, "but that doesn't mean that you have to hound me. What do you want now?"

"To be helpful," I said. "It is the duty of every citizen to help the police."

"There are several thousand men on the force. Why don't you spread your help around a little, instead of concentrating on me? Especially when I'm about to have my dinner."

"This'll only take a minute," I promised him. "I have a hunch, and who else can I go to with one? The rest of the force doesn't have your imagination or vision."

"I'd give you an answer to that, but my wife doesn't like me to swear when the kids are around. What is it, Milo?"

"They just found a body in the Hudson River up near Cornwall. No identification. He'd been shot, and they think he's been dead for about a week. It fits in with the time schedule on that job, and my hunch is that he's one of the gang. I thought you might be interested."

"I am," he said, "but I wish you'd get me interested during my on-duty hours, not afterwards. Where'd you say it was, Cornwall?"

"Near there. That's all the newspaper says. Get in touch with Lieutenant Paul Haynes at the State Police station in New Windsor. He's on the other case. If you give him what information you have on the men, he'll probably get an identification."

"Yes, sir," he said sarcastically. "Anything else, sir? Any other orders?"

"Sure. Go have your dinner."

"You mean you don't want me to call you back the minute I have any information?"

"No," I said cheerfully. "I wouldn't think of causing you any inconvenience. Good night, Johnny."

I went out and had my dinner. By the time I'd finished, I had made a decision. It was only an hour and a half to Cornwall. I'd drive up and be there in the morning. If I was right, I might be able to pick up some valuable information.

It was about an hour and fifteen minutes later when I passed through Cornwall. I stopped at the same motel as before and registered.

Then I went into town and had a few drinks at a neighborhood bar. I stopped in a liquor store and bought myself a bottle of V.O., and went back to the motel. I got some ice from the machine outside, undressed, turned on the TV set, and got into bed. I watched the idiot box until I was tired, and then went to sleep right in the middle of an old Clark Gable movie.

I was up early the next morning and drove into Cornwall for some breakfast. Then I went back down 9-W until I reached the New York State Police. The same sergeant was at the desk.

"Remember me?" I asked brightly. "I'd like to see Lieutenant Haynes."

He remembered me all right, but he wasn't going to admit it. "What's your name?" he asked.

"Milo March."

"What do you want to see the Lieutenant about?"

"The same thing I saw him about yesterday," I said with my most angelic smile.

He made some kind of noise under his breath, but he picked up the phone and grimly imparted the news that I was there. He replaced the phone and looked at me.

"You can go in," he said, but you could see his heart wasn't in it.

I walked back to the office and went in.

The Lieutenant glanced up from his desk. "I thought you left us yesterday morning, Mr. March," he said.

"I did, but I came back. I just can't resist these quaint old American towns. How are you, Lieutenant?"

"I'm fine," he said with a smile. "I'm afraid, however, that you're upsetting my sergeant. I don't think he approves of your attitude."

"That makes us even. I don't approve of his. We're all citizens, even those of us who aren't cops. Have you identified the man who was pulled out of the Hudson?"

The smile vanished from his face. "How did you know about that?" he asked.

"We live in a democratic country," I told him. "I read about it in the newspaper. I had a hunch, so I got in touch with Johnny Rockland on the New York police and suggested that he get in touch with you. I imagine he did."

"He had prints and mug shots of five men sent up last night. They were here this morning, and we got an identification about an hour ago."

"One of the five?"

He nodded. "A guy named George Dallin. He has quite a record. He was probably in on the robbery. We have a halfway identification of him as one of the men who set up the detour signs. It wouldn't stand up in court, but I think it's right."

"I thought it would be," I said. "Anything else on him or the others?"

"Not yet. I've had copies of the mug shots printed up and my men are going around to all the motels and hotels. I may have something later."

"I'll be in touch," I said.

I left, ignoring the Sergeant as I went by him. I drove into Cornwall and stopped at the bar I'd visited when I was there before. The owner wasn't in, so I had a couple of drinks and left. I stopped at a restaurant and had something to eat. Then I went back to the motel. I was restless. After a few minutes, I realized why. I wasn't going anywhere. I was sure that Lieutenant Haynes wouldn't come up with any information I could use. The most I could hope for from him was that he'd get the name of the motel where Dallin had stayed, and I already had that. There certainly wouldn't be any other clues left around.

Finally, I checked out of the motel and headed back for New York City, pushing the car as fast as the speed limit allowed. When I arrived, I parked on Perry Street and went up to my apartment. I poured myself a drink, lit a cigarette, and then worried some more. Then I picked up the phone and called Johnny Rockland.

"You're late," he said. "I was sure you'd be calling this

morning before I got the door open. The guy upstate was a pal of the one we pulled out of the East River."

"I know," I muttered.

"That's nice," he said. "Do you also know that he was killed with the same gun that killed Eddie Myers?"

"I didn't know that, but I could've guessed it. Whose gun?"

"How the hell do I know? We don't have a gun to check against the bullets."

"No news on the other three men and the girl?"

"No. Except that if you're right about the robbery, they're all a little richer."

"What're the records on the other three men?"

"I told you—everything from simple assault to armed robbery. You want it point by point?"

"I don't know what I want," I admitted. "I'm merely looking. There's one thing I'm sure of. They're on the run. But where?"

"Wait a minute," he said. "I've got the records here on my desk. ... You're probably right about them pulling the job upstate. We checked out the costume house. Then one of the group was killed down here and one was killed up there, both with the same gun. ... Here it is."

"Don't read them all to me. You're a smart cop. You must know what I'm looking for."

"Thanks," he said dryly. "Well ... there isn't too much to go on. Betty Bell was raised in Portsmouth, Ohio. Never got in any trouble there. Came to New York six years ago. Worked as a secretary until she met Peter Jackson. That was five years ago."

"They wouldn't head for there," I said. "That gang would stick out like a sore thumb in Portsmouth."

"Well, Dallin came from Flint, Michigan, and Eddie Myers was from Los Angeles. Both did time in their home states. But both are dead, so that probably doesn't help much."

"Not much."

"Jackson, Sforza, and Petrie were all born and raised in New York City. Wait a minute. … Well, there's only one other place mentioned in the records. George Dallin and Peter Jackson pulled a job together in Miami Beach two years ago. They were caught and both served one year in Florida."

"That's quite a selection," I said. "Are you sure the gang isn't lying low here in the city?"

"No, I'm not sure. I don't think they are. We've been looking pretty good since we found Myers."

"I don't think they're here either," I admitted. "One more thing, Johnny. Can I get copies of the mug shots?"

"I don't know why not," he said wearily. "I sometimes have the feeling that you're running the department anyway. Come down in about two hours and I'll have them for you." He hung up on me.

I was still restless. I had a cup of coffee, then a drink, and finally stretched out on the bed. I thought about the case and fell asleep.

I think I also dreamed about the case, but when I awakened, about an hour later, I didn't feel the least bit rested. I washed my face in cold water and went into the kitchen. I heated up the coffee and had a cup, staring blankly at the wall while I drank it.

Then, as I was getting ready to go downtown, I suddenly realized that I had made a decision, either just before I went to sleep or while I was asleep.

They had a million dollars in cash. Unmarked bills. The robbery had been well planned, so they weren't stupid. And unless they were, they would head for someplace where they'd have a fair chance of spending the money. There were a lot of places where they could go, but they had to get there.

I had made a decision. I was going to Florida—with the hope that it had been their jumping-off place.

THREE

Johnny Rockland was in the main building down on Centre Street. I took a cab there and went up to see him. Johnny's on the Special Squad, so he's always busy, but there was no one with him and he saw me right away. He was seated at his desk, which was piled high with paperwork. He looked up and smiled.

"Pretty soft," he said. "You insurance dicks really have it made. Draw a fat expense account, pick the brains of some poor cop, and then go out and have a ball."

"I'll remember that," I said, "the next time some guy is shooting at me. I used to wonder where all the cops were when the shooting started; then I discovered they were back at the office doing the paperwork. How are you, Johnny?"

He laughed. "How else? I'm a cop. Which means that I'm overworked, underpaid, and harassed by tax-paying citizens."

"That leaves me out. I never pay taxes unless I have to. How about the pictures?"

"Here they are." He tossed a manila envelope across the desk. He looked at me with a smile. "I suppose you'd better not tell me, because I'd have to share the information with the State Police, but I'd guess that you're heading for Florida."

"Why do you guess that?"

"Because that's what I'd do, if I had your case. Anyway, it's a nice place for a vacation. If you ever happen to go down there, give my regards to Lieutenant Dick Weston on the Miami Beach force. A nice guy."

"I'll do that—if I ever got down there," I said. "Thanks, Johnny."

I took my manila envelope and left.

I didn't look at the photographs until I got back to my apartment. Then I took them out and spread them across the table in my kitchen. Peter Jackson was a big, handsome man with dark hair. Sforza and Petrie were both dark, too, but small, with thin faces. Betty Bell was a slender but well-endowed blonde. Not even a police mug shot could conceal the fact that she was a doll.

I put the photographs away and went out. I had a couple of martinis and then a steak for dinner. After coffee, I went back to my apartment. I called and made a reservation on a plane for Miami the next morning. I thought of making a hotel reservation, but it wasn't the "season," so I decided there was no need for that. I called my telephone service. There were no messages. I told them that I would be out of town until further notice. I had a couple of drinks, watched some television, then read for an hour and went to bed.

I was up early the following morning. I had scrambled eggs, toast, and coffee at home, packed a suitcase, and left.

I had taken my passport just in case—you never knew when you might need it.

First I returned my rented car; then I took a taxi to Idlewild. I checked my baggage, picked up my ticket, and boarded the plane. I talked the stewardess into serving me a couple of martinis instead of coffee, then went back to sleep.

We were over the Florida coastline, just north of Miami, when I awakened. It was a clear day, and the landscape below looked like a jigsaw puzzle that had been put together too hastily.

We landed at the airport, and I took a taxi to the Hapsburg hotel on Collins Avenue in Miami Beach. It was about a forty-minute ride. The driver tried to give me a philosophical lecture on the women of Miami Beach, but I didn't pay much attention.

The Hapsburg House is like most of the plush hotels along Collins Avenue in Miami Beach. Its lobby looks like a large-scale European bawdy house, but its rooms are good and its food is fine and it has three very good bars. I checked in and got a room overlooking the ocean.

Thanks to the miracle of jets—which I can't stand—it was still early. I unpacked and went downstairs.

The main bar, just off the lobby, had barely opened., I went in, not so much because I wanted a drink but because one of my favorite bartenders worked there. His name was Buck Farrell. There was no one at the bar as I slipped quietly onto a stool. Buck's back was turned to me, and he was polishing glasses.

"Who do you have to know to get any service around here?" I asked.

He turned around and then his face lit up with a big smile as he recognized me.

"Hello, Mr. March," he said, coming over. Automatically, he started to make a martini. "When did you get in?"

"About ten minutes ago. How's everything, Buck?"

He rolled his eyes toward the ceiling, continuing to stir the martini. "Well, let's see … There's a good-looking blonde on the fourth floor and there's a brunette on the seventh who's a real doll. But I guess that's about it. The rest are dogs. But then you know how it is at nights. There are a lot of good-looking chicks who come into the bar. But no pros. You know how it is, Mr. March."

"I know," I admitted. "It's good to see you again, Buck."

He poured the martini. "Thank you, sir. It's good to see you again. A little vacation?"

I shook my head. "Work."

Buck knew all about my work, and a few times had provided valuable information. He seemed to know almost everything that was going on in the Beach area.

"Where's the blonde from?"

He dropped his voice to a confidential level. "Chicago. You looking for her, Mr. March?"

"Not if she's from Chicago," I said. "I'm looking for a blonde who's a dish. And there are three guys along. One of them, a big handsome guy, shacks up with the blonde. The other two are small. All three dark."

"When did they come down?"

"About a week ago. And they had plenty of money."

He shook his head. "I don't remember anyone like that. What's their racket?"

"Mostly armed robbery. And they don't have to practice it for a while."

"I don't think I've seen them, and I haven't heard about any hoods being in town. New ones, I mean. I'll ask around."

"Thanks, Buck. I'll be here for a day or two—until I get a lead to some other place."

I finished the martini, told Buck I'd see him later, and left. I took a cab downtown to the police station. I went in and asked for Lieutenant Weston. After a short wait I was shown into his office. He was a young fellow who, except for the uniform and a certain sharpness in his eyes, looked like a local accountant.

"What can I do for you, Mr. March?" he asked as I entered.

"I don't know," I said honestly. 'I'm a friend of Johnny Rockland in New York. He suggested that I look you up."

"Cop?" he asked. His manner had changed.

"In a way. I'm an insurance investigator, Intercontinental Insurance in New York." I pulled out my wallet and showed him my identification.

"Oh," he said. Then he waited to hear my side of it.

"I'm interested in three men and a girl. One of the men did time down here—two years ago. He served a year. I've got mug shots of all of them." I pulled the pictures from the manila envelope and put them on his desk.

He stared at them for a minute, then swung around and looked out the window.

Finally, he turned back and put a finger on the picture of Jackson. "I remember that one. His name is Johnson—no, Jackson. He was involved with another guy from New York. I think his name was Dallin or something like that. I don't know about him, but there's a bulletin out on Jackson from New York now. I got it this morning."

That caught me by surprise. Johnny Rockland and the State

Police lieutenant must've had conversations I didn't know about. I could only look my surprise.

Weston smiled and reached for a sheet on his desk. "From the New York State Police," he said. "Peter Jackson, Joseph Sforza, Tony Petrie, and Betty Bell wanted for questioning on suspicion of robbing an armored truck and of the murder of two guards. That who you're looking for?"

"They're the ones," I admitted, "but I didn't know there was a bulletin out on them yet."

"That's a nice bunch of cash they got," he said, glancing at the sheet again. "What makes you think they came down here?"

"Nothing but a hunch. Maybe they didn't come this way. But Jackson was familiar with this part of the country, and they might have."

"I guess that's right," he said. "But they could come here and mind their business and we might never hear of them. In fact, I haven't heard of Jackson since he was turned loose a year ago. You think they're holed up down here somewhere?"

"I don't know," I said. "I'm just looking. What was Jackson sent up for two years ago?"

"Robbery. He had a good lawyer and he got off light. So did his partner, that Dallin. I don't see his name here."

"That's because he's on a slab in New York State. Somebody put a few bullets in him and dumped him in the Hudson River."

He nodded. "You said you're an insurance investigator. How come you're interested in this case?"

"My company carried the insurance on the one million

dollars the armored truck was carrying, also on the bonds. Where did that old robbery of Jackson's take place?"

"Here in Miami Beach."

"Jackson hung out here, too?"

"No. He had a little shack up in Hollywood." The Lieutenant stopped and looked at me. "When did you say you thought Jackson might have come down this time?"

"A week ago—give or take a day."

He picked up his phone and pressed a button. "Jake," he said, "give me what we have on Howard Brock. ... Yeah, that's the one." He waited, drumming on the desk with his fingers. "Yeah?" he said, and then listened. When he'd heard enough, he hung up. He drummed some more before he looked at me. "How'd you like to take a ride with me?"

"Fine," I said.

He got up without saying any more, and I followed him out of the office. He picked one of the police cars in the parking lot and drove out into Collins Avenue, heading north. I sat beside him and waited. I figured that he'd tell me what was on his mind whenever he was ready.

"I don't have any jurisdiction in Hollywood," he said finally, "but I thought we'd take a ride up there. I just remembered something."

"What?" I asked.

"Five days ago there was an unsolved murder in Hollywood—a man named Howard Brock. I didn't pay any attention at the time. But I just checked on his record. He was in prison here at the same time that your Peter Jackson was. Same prison."

"How was this Brock killed?"

"Shot. They took two .38 bullets out of him."

I felt a new surge of excitement. Sure, there are a lot of guns of that caliber in the country, but there were too many coincidences. I don't believe in them.

"Sounds interesting," I said. "What did this Brock do, the same line of work?"

"So far as we know, he's been going straight since he got out a year ago. He's been a part-time fisherman since then. Maybe there's some connection, maybe not."

"It's worth looking into," I agreed.

It's a short drive from Miami Beach to Hollywood, and we were there in about twenty minutes. We parked in front of the police station and went in to see the local captain. He and Weston knew each other. Weston introduced me without telling him why I was along.

"I'm curious about a case of yours," Weston told him. "That killing of Howard Brock."

"That's a weird one, all right," the Captain said. "We ain't got a thing on it. Old Brock was going straight since he got out, and everybody liked him."

"Somebody didn't," Weston said.

"That's for sure. But I can't figure anybody who'd kill him. He didn't have any money to speak of. Only thing I can figure is maybe somebody had a grudge against him from before. A stranger."

"Any reports of strangers in town?"

"Not a one. Of course, he could've just slipped into town, done the killing, and slipped out again. That way, probably no one would've noticed."

Weston nodded. "Where'd Brock live?"

"In a shack out west of town. There are five little shacks there just at the edge of the city limits. Brock lived in the brown one."

"Do you mind," Weston asked, "if I go out there and ask a few questions?"

"Go right ahead," the Captain said. "Want me to come along with you?"

"I know you're busy, Captain, and I don't want to waste your time. We'll just look around, and if we stumble into anything we'll let you know."

"Fine," the Captain said.

We went out and the Lieutenant drove west out of town. As we reached the city limits, we spotted the cluster of shacks. We parked in front of the brown one and sat for a minute in the car.

"Looks like there are people home in the others," the Lieutenant said.

"Let's try the one next to him."

We got out and went up to the house. He knocked on the door.

After a while we heard a shuffling inside and then the door opened. A woman stood there, a thin slattern of a woman in a loose, worn dress, her face wrinkled and her mouth bitter. Her gaze swept over us and then went past us to the police car.

"If'n the landlord sent you," she said, "you-all can tell him my husband is on his way with the money."

"We don't know anything about your landlord," the Lieutenant said. "We want to ask you some questions about Howard Brock, who lived next door."

Her mouth tightened even more. "We done told the police chief everything we knowed."

"I'm sure you did," Weston said. "We just want to ask you a few questions."

"Go ahead and ask." Her tone indicated that to her, police questions only meant trouble.

"Did you know Howard Brock?"

"I knowed him."

"Did you know any of his friends?"

"He didn't have none. Leastways, no callin' friends. Maybe he had friends in the bar down the street. We already told the chief there wasn't nobody around last week."

"What about before that?" I asked.

She examined me before she answered. "Who's going to be friends with anybody livin' in these shacks? We been here for a year, and he never had no visitors—'cept that once maybe a month ago."

The Lieutenant and I exchanged glances.

"Who was that?" he asked.

She shrugged. "Two men. City folks. Yankees. That's all I know."

"Did you tell the chief about them?"

"He didn't ask."

"What were they doing here?"

"I don't know. Up to no good, I expect."

"Why do you say that?"

"What'd they be doin' in a place like this? Anyways, when they left, Brock was bragging to my old man that he was going to have plenty of money. Nobody was going to pay him plenty of money for any honest work. And it wasn't fishin'. I've been hearin' about plenty of money from that for ten years, but I ain't seen none of it."

"You saw both of the men?" Weston asked.

"I seen them."

He looked at me. I took the picture of Peter Jackson from the envelope and held it up. She squinted at it.

"That's one of them," she said. "Fancy dressed, he was— and a fancy car. Now, what would he be doing with the likes of Brock?"

"And he wasn't back within the last week?" I asked.

"Not that I seen. Maybe they come in the middle of the night when honest folks was asleep."

"Well, thank you very much," the Lieutenant said. We turned away as she slammed the door.

We tried the other houses. We got essentially the same story at three of them. A man in the fourth house slammed the door in our faces before we could even tell him what we wanted. We went to the police car and headed back the way we had come.

"Well," the Lieutenant said, after we had driven several blocks, "I guess your man was here."

"Yeah. Four weeks ago. So it's a good guess that Brock was somehow used in the escape plan and then killed so he couldn't tell anyone else. And the second man was probably Dallin, who's already dead. Jackson is a very neat man."

"Too much so," the Lieutenant said.

"What now?" I asked.

"Nothing you can bet your life savings on. The New York

State Police sent me pictures and I already ordered copies. I'll get them out. I'll send a man out to the airport and cover the trains and buses. We'll also try to cover any ships that have sailed, and small planes that are for charter. Then we wait, but don't hold your breath."

"I never do," I said.

"I'll let you know as soon as I get anything. Where are you staying?"

"Hapsburg House."

"I'll drop you off as we go by. And I'll keep in touch."

"Okay," I said.

I had my own idea about the case, but I decided to keep it to myself.

He let me out in front of the hotel. I went inside and headed for the bar. Buck was there and came over at once to mix a martini.

"I didn't hear anything yet," he said.

"I didn't hear much myself," I said. I waited until he put the martini in front of me. Then I took out the picture of Peter Jackson. "Ever see this guy, Buck?"

He studied the picture for a minute, then shook his head. "I don't think so. If I did, I guess he didn't make any impression. I don't remember him."

"It was just a wild stab," I said. "I don't think he was here very long. Thanks anyway, Buck."

He nodded, rubbing the bar with a cloth. "You staying long, Mr. March?"

"I don't know," I said. "Probably not."

"But you'll be staying overnight?"

"I imagine so. Why?"

"Just wondered," he said.

I had another martini and then went into the dining room for lunch. While I ate, I thought about the case. The more I thought, the more I felt there should be a lead through the Howard Brock case. When I'd finished lunch, I went to the desk and told them I wanted to rent a car. They promised there'd be one at the door within a half hour. I went back to the bar and had a stinger for dessert.

It was a little less than a half hour when I was paged. I went out and the car was there. It was a new Ford. I signed for it and climbed in. I headed back for Hollywood.

When I reached it, I followed the same route Weston and I had taken. I remembered that the woman had mentioned a bar down the street, so as I neared the shacks, I kept a sharp watch for it. There was only one, and it was about three blocks from where Brock had lived. I pulled in and parked in the space beside the building. I locked the car and went in.

It was a typical neighborhood bar in an area where there wasn't much work.

Everything was fly-specked, including the shuffleboard and the jukebox. There were seven men sitting at the bar, most of them drinking beer.

The bartender was tall, thin, and cadaverous, and looked as if he were tired of the whole business.

I took a stool near the other men at the bar and ordered a whiskey and soda backed.

"Have one yourself and give the bar a drink," I said when he brought mine. I put a five-dollar bill on the bar.

"Don't mind if we do," the bartender said. He served the

drinks, including a bottle of beer for himself. He took my money and brought my change. I figured out the prices were about right. Forty cents for whiskey, fifteen cents for a glass of beer, and twenty-five cents for a bottle of beer.

"The stranger bought the drinks," the bartender said flatly. He raised his glass.

"Good luck," I said.

The bartender swallowed some of his beer and looked at me. "From up North?" he asked.

"Yes," I admitted.

"We don't get many of them out here," he said.

"I suppose not," I said.

"We don't get any of them that buy drinks for the bar," he said. He stared at me for a minute. "The way I look at it, you must want something."

"I want something," I said.

"What?"

I finished my drink and indicated a refill. The bar was silent while he gave it to me. "A man was killed here a few days ago," I said then. "I didn't know him. But I want the man who killed him."

"You mean Howie Brock?" one of the men asked.

"That's who I mean."

"Cop?" the bartender asked.

"I didn't say I wanted to arrest the man who killed Brock. I said I wanted the man who killed him."

"Why?"

I smiled. "That is my business. You have things that are your business and I have things that are mine." There was a moment of silence while the bartender and the men at the bar looked at each other. I worked on my drink and waited.

"What do you want to know?" the bartender asked after their silent communication was finished.

I relaxed. I had taken a gamble and it looked as if I might have won.

"About four weeks ago Brock had two visitors. One of them was a big guy—dark hair, and you might call him good-looking. The other one was a little blond guy, chunky."

"Yeah," the bartender said. "They were in here with him. They were buying him a lot of drinks, but not anybody else."

I nodded. "Sounds like them. Was the big, dark one back just before Brock was killed?"

"We didn't see him," the bartender said. By some silent agreement, he was apparently elected the spokesman. "How come you don't ask about the other guy?"

"He's on a slab in New York City."

"Well," he said, "the two fellows come down here, like you said, about a month ago. We don't know what they were doing here. But Howie started bragging as soon as they left that he was going to make a lot of money. We didn't pay much attention. Howie always was one for big talk. We didn't think no more about it until he was killed. Then we thought that maybe Howie wasn't just talking."

"That's all you know?"

"That's about it."

I ordered another round of drinks for everyone and waited until they were served and the bartender had collected his money.

"Well, that's the way it goes," I said. "Did Brock hang out in any other bar?"

"I think he did. Some joint over near the ocean, but I don't know what it was." He glanced at the men along the bar.

"Maybe there's something," one of the men said. "Howie kept talkin' about Bill Jemson. But I didn't think Howie would know him, so I didn't pay much attention."

"Who's Bill Jemson?" I asked.

"He rents out boats for the rich people who come down and want to go after big fish. Jemson's pretty rich himself by this time, so I didn't think him and Howie would have much to do with each other. But Howie was stiff a couple of nights and kept talking about his meetings with Jemson. Come to think of it, it was right after them two fellows was here."

"Where do you find this Jemson?" I asked.

"He's got a place right below the Hollywood Hotel," the bartender said.

"But maybe Howie was just talking to himself. I wouldn't put it past him."

"Maybe," I said. I looked at the change on the bar and told him to give everybody another round. I finished my own drink and went out to the car. I drove back into the city and on to the ocean. I didn't have any trouble finding the place. It was a dock, where several boats were tied up, and a two-room office with a sign that announced *Jemson's Boats*.

I parked the car and went in. There was a girl behind the desk, a pretty girl.

"Yes?" she asked.

"I wanted to see Mr. Jemson," I said.

"He's not here at the moment. Did you want to charter a boat?"

"Not exactly. It's more of a personal matter."

"Oh," she said. She studied me for a minute. "He's probably in the bar at the hotel."

"Thank you," I said. I turned and walked out.

I drove up to the hotel. I parked and went into the bar. There were only three people there besides the bartender, all men. I went up and picked a stool in the middle. I ordered a whiskey and soda backed and waited until the bartender brought me my change.

"I was told by his office that Mr. Jemson was here," I said.

He nodded his head to the right. "That's him at the end of the bar."

"Thanks," I said.

I picked up my drink and walked to the end of the bar. I put the drink down and climbed on the stool next to him. He was a short, heavyset man with gray hair—well dressed. Not on his first drink, if I knew the signs.

"Mr. Jemson?" I said.

He looked at me for the first time. "Yes," he said, as though he had no interest in why I asked.

"A very pretty girl in your office told me that I might find you here."

"The very pretty girl is my daughter and she has a big mouth. If you want to charter a boat, she's perfectly capable of handling the transaction."

"I don't want to charter a boat."

He sighed and took a closer look at me. "Cop?"

"No."

"Then what do you want to talk about?"

"Howard Brock. I think some people called him Howie."

This time his sigh was heavier. "You knew Brock?"

"No. But I want to find the man that killed him."

"You're not a cop?"

"No."

He looked disappointed. "I've been going out of my mind," he said. "Should I call the police, should I keep quiet, or what?"

I kept quiet and sipped at my drink.

"Well," he said finally, "I guess the questions have been answered for me. ... I knew Brock—only by sight until very recently. He was another one of the part-time fishermen, making maybe forty or fifty dollars a month."

"And then recently?" I prodded.

"Well, it's funny," he said. "About a month ago Brock came to me. Said he'd made some money and he wanted to buy one of my boats. I didn't really want to sell, but he kept insisting, so I finally put a price on it—fifteen thousand dollars. At least three more than it was worth. He said he'd take it, and he gave me a thousand dollars as a down payment. Frankly, I was surprised that he had a thousand dollars, and I didn't think he'd ever come up with the rest of it. I put the money in my safe, figuring I'd give it back to him when he came around and said he couldn't pay the rest of it."

"But he did come around with the rest," I said.

He nodded. "Six days ago he showed up with fourteen thousand dollars. The day before he was killed."

"You sold him the boat?"

"I'd agreed to. Sure I did."

"Then what happened?"

"He said that four of his friends were going to take the boat out fishing the next morning. They did, too. But they never came back. And that afternoon I heard that Brock had been killed."

"What did the friends look like?"

"A big guy and two little guys—all dark. And a blond girl, a dish. You know what I mean?"

"I know what you mean. They give you any names?"

"No names. Just friends of Howie Brock. They were supposed to be back that same night. That's the last I heard of them, or the boat."

"What kind of a boat was it? Seaworthy?"

"Sure. You could cross the ocean if you didn't mind living recklessly. It was fifty feet, twin engines, everything in ship-shape order."

"How did he pay you? Cash?"

"Cash. One-hundred-dollar bills. I shouldn't have taken it. I never knew Howie Brock to have a hundred dollars in his life. But there it was, and I had promised I'd sell him the boat. And I've been worrying ever since. What do you think I should do?"

"Notify the Coast Guard," I said. "Maybe they're in trouble."

"If they were in trouble six days ago, now they got more trouble than you can imagine."

"Then don't tell them."

"That's not so easy either. I gave Brock a proper bill of sale, but they apparently didn't find it when they found him. So what do I say when it's found, or even if I go to them now?"

"You've got me there," I admitted. I finished my drink and slid off the stool. "Well, thanks, Mr. Jemson."

"Sure," he said glumly. "What did you say your name was?"

"I didn't say. But it's Milo March."

"I don't know why I asked," he said. "It doesn't help my problem any."

"So just keep quiet," I told him. "You've played it this way for six days; you might as well go the route."

"Yeah," he said. He was staring at the drink in front of him. "That's easy to say. What are you going to do, March?"

"Me?" I said. "I'm going to follow a runaway boat—even though I can't swim."

FOUR

It was about three o'clock when I got back to the hotel. I turned in the car and paid for it. I bought a couple of maps and went up to my room. I studied the maps for about a half hour. I didn't think there were too many places they'd try to go in the boat they'd bought. Finally, I decided where. It was near enough and it was probably safe for them. No one would think of them heading for Cuba. But from Havana they could get a plane to almost any other country. They had to worry about bulletins and they also had to worry about extradition, so Cuba was a logical choice.

I put down the maps and picked up the phone. I put through a call to Martin Raymond. I just had time to catch him, and I made it.

"Milo, boy," he said a minute later. "Where are you?"

"Miami Beach," I said.

"What's going on?"

"I need some money."

There was a short pause. Then he gave a Madison Avenue–type laugh. "The price of martinis go up?"

"No, but the price of traveling did. It's easier to get the money here than when I get out of the country."

"Oh," he said. "How much do you want?"

"You'd better send me another two thousand in care of the

Hapsburg House so I'll get it in the morning. I want to leave as early as I can get a reservation."

"Where are you going?"

"South," I said.

His breathing sounded as if he were having a heart attack. "All right," he said. "I'll send it out before I leave tonight."

"That's my boy," I said, and hung up.

I took a nap and then went downstairs about six-thirty. Buck saw me coming and indicated that I should sit right in front of where he was standing. I walked over and slid on the stool. Then I became aware of the perfume. It reached out and put its arms around me. I looked to see where it was coming from, and suddenly I had trouble breathing. She was tall, stacked, dark, and beautiful. I had a hunch about her. I looked at Buck. I was right. He was beaming.

"Miss Sherwood," he said, "I'd like you to meet Mr. March."

She looked at me with a little smile. "Hello, Mr. March," she said.

"Hello, Miss Sherwood," I said gravely. "Buck spent a good part of the day telling me about you. But you know, he understated your case."

She laughed. "He's been spending the evening telling me about you."

"Well, Buck," I said, "I think the least you can do is give both of us a drink."

"Sure, Mr. March," he said, and went happily to work.

"I've never been able to figure out about Buck," I said. "He's either a frustrated marriage broker or a frustrated white slaver."

She laughed again.

"My name is Milo," I added.

"Mine is Elaine," she said.

So we had a couple of drinks and talked and slowly got acquainted. She was everything Buck had said she was—especially a doll. After the drinks, she agreed to have dinner with me, and we went into the dining room. Buck watched us go with the happy expression of a father who has just married off his oldest daughter.

We had two more drinks before they brought dinner, and it was then that I was paged. The waiter brought over a telephone and plugged it into a wall outlet.

"Hello," I said.

"Hi, Milo. This is Johnny Rockland."

"Johnny," I said in surprise. "Where are you?"

"New York. You may remember that I work here."

"And you're spending the taxpayer's money to call me. I'm flattered."

"Not so loud," he said. "They don't mind me spending the money, but if they knew I spent it on you, I might be suspended."

"How did you know where to find me?"

"I just called Martin Raymond and he told me. He also told me that you're heading south."

"That's the general idea."

"Any particular spot?"

"Not exactly. I want to check every place within easy travel distance by a fishing boat."

"They took off from there in one?"

"Yes."

"I have some information," he said, "which may help. It'll probably be in the papers tomorrow. Tony Petrie is dead now."

"Where?"

"He was found in a boat in Cuban waters, just off of Havana."

"The others?"

"No mention of them. They probably got out of Cuba before the body was found."

"How? I thought it was impossible to get in and out."

"You surprise me, Milo. You can get in and out of almost any country if you have the money and see the proper person. They certainly had the money."

"Yeah," I said. "That was all the news?"

"That was it. Castro made a speech and said it indicated that another group of CIA agents were invading Cuba. He said that they must have had an argument and the others killed this one. He reported that they were searching Cuba for the other agents."

"Okay. Thanks, Johnny."

"Just part of our service," he said, and hung up.

I put the phone down and the waiter carried it away. I turned to the girl. "Sorry for the interruption."

"That's all right. Did I hear you say you were leaving?"

"Probably tomorrow morning," I said.

"Where are you going?'

"I don't know yet."

"Oh," she said. "You mean you'd rather not tell a complete stranger."

"Honey, you're not a stranger—although you are complete. Remember that Buck introduced us."

She laughed. "He's funny, isn't he?"

"Not only funny, but a man of impeccable taste. He said you were a doll and he was right."

"You should hear what he said about you."

"No, I shouldn't. It would only go to my head. It's better that I stay my own simple, humble self."

She laughed again, and I decided that maybe her brain wasn't so great—but the rest of her was.

After dinner we went to the Flamingo Room. We were just in time to catch the show. Afterwards we had a few drinks and danced until two in the morning. Then I took her upstairs.

"It was a nice evening," I told her in front of her door. "I'm sorry I have to leave in the morning."

"Room service is still open," she said. "Would you like to come in for a nightcap? And you can tell me why you have to go away as soon as I've met you."

"Best offer I've had all day," I said, and followed her into the room.

It was quite a nightcap. We never did get around to talking about why I was leaving.

I was up early the next morning. I had breakfast in my room, then went downstairs. I got a map from the travel agent and returned to my room. I went over it carefully. There was only one place that made any sense; only one place to go if you had a million dollars and were wanted by the American police. That was Brazil. They had no extradition treaty with us, and it had long been a haven for American crooks who were loaded with loot.*

I picked up the phone and called the travel agent. "This is March in 618," I said. "I'd like you to put me on the first available plane to Rio de Janeiro."

"I'll see what I can get and call you back."

I studied the map some more and felt surer that I was right. I folded up the map and waited. The phone rang in a few minutes. I picked it up and said hello.

"Mr. March," the travel agent said, "there's a Brazilian jet leaving Miami in a little less than an hour. There is an available seat and you can just make it if you want to."

"Make out the ticket. I'll be right down."

I packed quickly and carried my bag downstairs without waiting for a bellboy. I paid the agent and picked up my ticket. Then I took a taxi to the airport.

They started loading shortly after I'd arrived. I checked my bag, showed my passport, and went aboard. I made myself comfortable and went to sleep even before the plane took off.

I awakened once to have a couple of martinis and some lunch, and then I went back to sleep. Even when I'm not tired I usually do that. To me, a plane is like a bus up in the air, and one cloud looks like another, so this is the best way to handle it.

I didn't awaken again until about a half hour before arrival time. I had only been to Rio de Janeiro once before, but I still remembered it as one of the beautiful cities of the world. The airport is on Guanabara Bay, and as we glided into the land-

* As of December 1964—just months after this book was first published—Brazil's extradition treaty with the United States went into effect. However, Brazil does not extradite its own citizens.

ing strip the sun was just setting and lights were coming on along the streets near the bay and the seashore.

The floodlights had already been turned on, bathing the huge statue of Christ the Redeemer on the peak of Corcovado. It was a beautiful sight. I could tell by the way conversation stopped that even the natives had never become bored by the sight of their city.

I went through customs without any trouble at all. I was a little worried about the gun, but my suitcase was small and the inspector pawed at a couple of shirts, then snapped it shut. He wished me a happy stay in Brazil and I was through.

I stopped outside and found a public phone. Then I had a problem about money.

But I soon found a place that would exchange some of my dollars for me. I went back to the booth and had the operator connect me with the Copacabana Palace Hotel on the beach. I'd decided that since Intercontinental was paying the bill, I might as well live comfortably. A few minutes later I had a reservation. I went out, found a taxi, and told the driver where to take me.

It was a nice ride, first around the bay and then along Avenida Atlantica until we reached the Copacabana Palace Hotel. I went in and registered. The clerk changed some more money for me and a bellhop took me up to my room. It turned out to be a very nice little home away from home. If I could have sent a picture of it to Martin Raymond, he would have had a heart attack.

Which reminded me that it was two hours earlier in New York than it was in Rio de Janeiro. With luck he'd still be in his office. I picked up the phone and put through a collect call.

There was a lot of conversation between operators, most of it spent on trying to understand each other, and finally Martin Raymond was on the phone.

"Milo," he said, "where are you?"

"Rio de Janeiro," I said.

"What the hell are you doing there?"

"Remember, I'm on a job for you. Or had you forgotten?"

"You mean they're there?"

"I think they came here. I just got in, so I haven't had a chance to check on it yet."

"You mean that's all you have to report? And that's why you telephoned?"

"No," I said cheerfully. "I phoned to tell you to send me some more money."

"What?" he said. It sounded like the scream of a wounded animal. "You've been on the job only a few days and I've given you four thousand dollars. What are you doing with it?"

"Spending it," I said. "You know, once I get abroad I am the image of Intercontinental, and you wouldn't want me to tarnish it, would you?"

"All right," he said wearily. "Tell me what's going on."

"Three of the original six are dead," I said. "One in New York near West Point, one in New York City. The trail led from New York to Miami Beach, Florida. They bought a boat and took off in it. It was not really large enough to cross the ocean, so I guessed they'd head for Cuba."

"Why?"

"Simple. The police wouldn't think of looking there for them, and wouldn't get any cooperation if they did. And they probably thought they had enough money to get them out of Cuba. I think they did. But one more member died there."

"How did you learn all this?"

"From a member of the New York police. But I'll give you an accounting of the money when I get back—unless you'd like me to itemize it now."

"No, thanks, not at these rates. How much do you want?"

"Better send me at least two thousand. I may have to spread some down here, too. Send it to me at the Copacabana Palace Hotel."

He groaned. "You couldn't find a hotel with more moderate rates?" he asked sarcastically.

"And have everyone think Intercontinental is going broke?"

"We will be if you work for us long enough. All right, all right. I'll send it to you."

"Think how small it is compared with a million dollars."

"Just one thing. Brazil has no extradition agreement with us. What do you intend to do about that?"

"I don't know yet," I said cheerfully, "but I'll think of something. That's what you're paying me for."

"It better be," he said grimly. He hung up.

I waited a couple of minutes, then picked up the phone again. I asked for room service, and when they answered I ordered a double martini in my best Portuguese.

It came in about ten minutes. I paid and tipped the waiter. As soon as he was gone, I stripped off all my clothes and stretched out on the bed. I sipped the martini slowly, enjoying every taste of it. Finally, when it was all gone, I unpacked my shaving stuff and carried it into the bathroom. I shaved, then took a long shower.

I examined my second suit; it looked in pretty good condition. I got dressed and went downstairs. I decided to try the hotel dining room for dinner, but later I wanted to move out to places where I could get a better sample of local food. I stopped in the lobby and bought a newspaper, then went on into the dining room. I picked a table in the corner, ordered another martini, and started wading through the paper. I was able to read most of it easily, although occasionally I had to puzzle over a word. I had an excellent steak for dinner and finally walked out about an hour later.

I went outside and shook my head at the doorman who wanted to get me a taxi. I walked down the Avenida a way, then cut over to the beach. The water was calm and lovely, and there were a few swimmers splashing around. I stood there for several minutes and then walked a few more blocks. But I didn't know where I was going and actually didn't feel like doing much of anything, so I soon turned back to the hotel. I went into the main bar and had a drink. It was moderately crowded. Around the bar I could hear several languages being spoken.

I stayed in the bar for a couple of hours, drinking slowly, then went up to my room. I got undressed, turned on the radio, and got into bed. I was still tired, despite my nap on the plane, and it wasn't long before I'd drifted off.

The radio was still on when I awakened early the next morning. I phoned room service and ordered breakfast.

I also phoned the valet service and asked them to pick up some laundry and a suit. Both services arrived about the same time. I gave out the laundry and asked them to mark it rush. I sent the suit to be pressed. Then I sat down to a breakfast of papaya, eggs and ham, and a pot of the best coffee I'd had in a long time.

When I was dressed, I walked out on the balcony. My room faced the ocean and I had an unobstructed view in three directions. I've never seen anything like it anywhere. The ocean itself was several different colors; then there was the white sand, already covered with a rainbow of swimsuits and umbrellas. On the other two sides there was nothing but lush green, generously dotted with the brilliant colors of birds, butterflies, and flowers.

Finally, I turned and went back into the room, which now seemed drab and sullen after the view from the balcony. I went out and took the elevator downstairs. The doorman waved his arms at my nod and a taxi pulled up for me. I climbed in. The driver turned to look at me.

I had a glimpse of a dark face and bright, merry eyes. "Where to, Senhor?" he asked.

"Police headquarters," I told him.

The driver gave me a startled look. He turned to have a better look at me.

"There is something wrong, Senhor?"

"Nothing wrong," I said. "I merely want to go to police headquarters for information."

He made a clicking sound with his tongue and we drove off. "The Senhor is a foreigner?"

"Yes."

"I could tell it from the way the Senhor speaks our language." He chuckled to show that he appreciated his own shrewdness. "You are Spanish, no?"

"No. I speak Spanish, but I am an American."

"I would never have guessed," he exclaimed. "You like Cidade Maravilhosa?" This was a local name—meaning the Marvelous City—for Rio.

"Very much."

"Now you can see why it is God's favorite spot and why He spent so much time on it."

"How's that?" I asked.

He narrowly missed a pedestrian and ignored the shout that came from behind us.

"You do not know?" He shook his head at my ignorance. "You do know that it is written that God created the earth and Heaven in six days?"

"Yes."

"Well, it is not written, but if you ask any *carioca* he will tell you that God devoted two days to making Rio and four days to the rest of the world. … Tell me, Senhor, does it cost much to come here from your country?"

"Several hundred dollars."

"Think of that," he said. He chuckled. "You see, I am here and it cost nothing but some small pains to my mother."

"You like it better here than anywhere else?"

He nodded his head violently. "Yes. And I have been other places, not like the others here—unless they are rich. I worked on the ships, but I could never wait to get back to Rio. Then one day I decided to stay, and here I am."

"Have you been driving a taxi long?"

"Four years, Senhor."

"Does it pay you well?"

He shrugged. "It is not bad. On a good day I may make as much as twenty-four hundred cruzeiros. Other days, perhaps eighteen hundred. It is mostly tourists. Anyone living in Rio, if he has enough money to take a taxi, will buy a car and not need a taxi."

"Is that enough to live on?"

"Very well, Senhor. We have a little house in the *favelas*. We have two goats who give us milk, and twice a year we have young goat meat. And we have chickens who give us eggs and sometimes of their meat. So you see we manage to save money so that our two children may go to school when they are grown. Who knows, they might be engineers or lawyers someday."

"Tell me," I said, "what would you do if I were to pay you in American money? Take it to the bank to exchange it?"

"Oh, no, Senhor. They would give me only six hundred cruzeiros for one dollar.

I would take it to the men in the streets, who will give me eleven hundred cruzeiros. Sometimes I make extra money because passengers pay me in the money of their country. But not as much as when it is in dollars." He pulled the cab to a lurching stop in front of a large ornate building. "We have arrived, Senhor."

I took a dollar bill from my pocket and handed it up to the driver. "I know that the fare is no more than half of this, but you may keep all of it."

"Obrigado," he said.

"How are you called?" I asked.

"Alcino Campos."

"I don't know how long I will stay in Rio, Alcino, but how would you like to work for me every day that I'm here?"

"What would I do, Senhor?"

"Drive your taxi. You would come to the hotel each morning and wait for me. You would drive me wherever I want to go and wait for me. You would drive no other passengers."

He thought about it.

"For this," I went on, "I will pay you at the end of each day four dollars in American money."

He was quiet while he worked out the mathematics. Then he smiled. "I will do it. How are you called, Senhor?"

"My name is Milo March."

"When do I start, Senhor March?"

"You already have," I said with a smile. "Consider the dollar I gave you as money you earned before you started to work for me. In the meantime, wait here for me."

"I will be here, Senhor."

I got out of the taxi and went into the building. There was a policeman at a desk just inside the door. I explained to him the best I could that I wanted to see whoever was in charge of the department that concerned itself with foreigners in Rio de Janeiro. After I had said my piece about three times, his face lit up with understanding.

"That is Lieutenant Floriano Alvares. The second floor, first door to the right."

"Thank you."

"Your name and country, Senhor?"

"Milo March. The United States of America."

He laboriously wrote it down, then waved me to go ahead. I saw, as I was leaving, that he was reaching for the telephone.

I walked up the stairs and turned right. I stopped at the first door and knocked. A voice called for me to come in. I opened the door and looked in. There was a single man sitting in a small office.

"Lieutenant Alvares?" I asked.

"Come in, Senhor March," he said.

I stepped into the office, closing the door behind me. I noticed that he was looking me over, so I took advantage of the time to study him. I saw a tall, slender man, probably in his early forties. His uniform was immaculate, and his black hair was slicked down and had a shine like patent leather. His face was thin and sharp—almost like a ferret's. There was a shrewd look in his eyes when he glanced up. I had a feeling he'd been trying to estimate whether I had money or not.

"Please sit down," he said, indicating the chair beside his desk. He waited until I was seated. "What can I do for you, Senhor March?"

I smiled. "I see the man downstairs phoned you while I was on my way up."

He answered my smile. "Of course, Senhor. But that is not all that I know about you." He glanced at a sheet of paper on his desk. "I know that you are Senhor Milo March from New York City. I know that you arrived here last night on a Brazilian airliner from Miami, Florida, and that you are staying at the Copacabana Palace Hotel and that you brought very little luggage with you. I also know that you placed a phone call to New York City as soon as you were in your room. Unfortunately, I do not know what was said on the call." He made a little gesture with his hands, as though to apologize for not knowing that.

I made a mental note to make no more calls from the hotel, because I had the feeling he might try to rectify that oversight in the future.

"I am glad to see that you do your job so thoroughly, Lieutenant Alvares."

He acknowledged the compliment with a modest smile. "What can I do for you, Senhor?"

"I'm looking for three people, countrymen of mine. I think they came here by way of Cuba."

"Ah?" he said politely. "Are you perhaps a police officer from America?"

"Not the sort you are. I am a private detective."

"Like in the motion pictures?" he asked with a smile.

"There are a few similarities, but most of the time it is quite different."

He nodded. "Do you carry any special identification as a private detective?"

I nodded and took out my wallet. I removed my New York State license and spread it out for him. He bent over it for several minutes, then straightened up.

"Very interesting, Senhor March," he said. "These three persons you are following … what have they done?"

"Murder," I said. I decided not to mention the robbery. The Lieutenant had too hungry a look about him.

"No robbery with it?" he asked with another smile.

"I guess they took whatever money their victims were carrying, but none of those were rich, so I don't suppose it amounted to much."

"Strange. How do you suppose they managed to travel so far?"

"They were professional criminals. I imagine they had some money left from earlier jobs."

He was tapping his desk with a pencil. "Who were the victims?"

"Four other criminals who had sometimes worked with them and two truck drivers."

His eyebrows went up. "Truck drivers? Hauling valuable cargo?"

"No. They were transferring paper from one warehouse to another."

"Why should they kill them?"

"I don't know. Perhaps the truck drivers saw them trying to pull a robbery and were killed so there would be no witnesses."

"Yes, yes," he said. He smiled again. "Your country is known for its big criminals, Senhor March. Perhaps they were such as this?"

"I'm afraid not. They had gone to prison for such things as holding up grocery stores."

He made a face. "If they are so unimportant, why have you come so far in pursuit of them?"

"Because I'm being paid to," I said bluntly. "That's the way my business works. Someone hires me at my regular rates, and I try to do what they want."

"Who would want three murderers other than the regular police?"

"I never tell who my client is on a given case. Sometimes it's relatives of the criminal, sometimes relatives of the victim, sometimes merely a friend."

"And private detectives are permitted to work on murder cases in your country?"

"The authorities do not approve of it," I said with a smile, "but they can't stop me as long as I don't interfere with them or break any laws."

"Strange," he said. He snapped his fingers as though he had suddenly thought of something. "But I am impolite. You have been answering my questions and I have answered none of yours. What do you know of these three?"

"There are two men and a woman. Both men in their thirties. Both dark, but one is large and handsome, the other small. The girl is in her twenties, a pretty blonde. Since they needed passports, they are probably using their own names. The men are Peter Jackson and Joseph Sforza. The girl is Betty Bell. I have reason to believe that they were about five days ahead of me."

He tapped the pencil on the desk a few more times, then seemed to make a decision. He looked at me. "They are here under those names, Senhor March. The girl and Jackson are staying at the same hotel as you are, and are registered as husband and wife. Joseph Sforza is staying at the Copacabana Hill Hotel two blocks away. All three spend much of the day on the beach in front of your hotel, but not always together. At night, after dinner, they usually go to one of two clubs, neither far away. One is the Jogo do Bicho, named after our local lottery, and the other is Uma Figa. They seldom go anywhere else. They have lived well, but not lavishly, since arriving from Cuba just six days ago."

"Thank you, Lieutenant," I said.

"May I make a suggestion about your problem, Senhor March?"

"Surely."

"You must know, Senhor March, that there is no extradition treaty between your country and mine. We cannot arrest these persons unless they commit a crime in our country. If we had them under arrest, we could not return them to your country."

"I know that," I said.

"Should you try to force them back to your country, you yourself might be arrested for kidnapping."

"I'm also aware of that."

"On the other hand, if they have as little money as you seem to think, it will not be long before they have no more. Then, one of two things will happen. They may try to get money by committing crimes in Brazil. If they do that, we will arrest them and they will go to prison here instead of your country. If they don't commit a crime and they have no money, they will undoubtedly be deported back to your country, and you can get them when they land. I suggest that you return home and have patience."

"You're probably right," I said. "But I think I'll stick around a few days and try to talk to them."

"About what?"

"I'll have to try to talk them into going back voluntarily. It's my job. And I won't mind a few days of seeing your beautiful city."

He shrugged. "I wish you luck, Senhor March." It was clearly a dismissal.

I got up and went to the door. "Well, thanks again, Lieutenant. By the way, I've noticed that you're a very thorough worker, so if you'd like to check up on me, you might get in touch with Lieutenant John Rockland, New York City Police Department."

He smiled. "Thank you. If there's anything I can do for you, call on me, Senhor March."

I nodded and left.

Alcino was still waiting in his taxi. I opened the door and got in.

"Ah, Senhor," he said, "I was afraid that they might have decided to keep you."

"I think the Lieutenant might have liked that, but he decided to give me my information in the hope that he might find an advantage later on. He is a hungry one."

"Who did you see?"

"Lieutenant Alvares."

He made a face. "Alvares! That one has his hands in everybody's pockets except his own, and they are too full. … Where now, Senhor?"

"Back to the hotel, I think."

He nodded and pulled away from the curb. I looked through the back window and saw a small Italian car pull out right behind us.

"I think we are being followed, Alcino."

"Yes, Senhor. I saw him. That is a car the police use when they want to think they are fooling people. I recognized it when I saw it parked there. Then a man came out and got into it just before you arrived. You want me to get away from him, Senhor?"

"No. Let him follow us. Just drive up to the front of the hotel and let me out. Then you drive on. You can take a few hours off. Come back for me at four o'clock. But come to the rear of the hotel, and I'll meet you there. That way we'll leave our watchdog still waiting out front."

He grinned with delight. "But won't you need me before then, Senhor?"

"No. I'm going swimming. Do whatever you want to, and I'll meet you at four o'clock."

He nodded.

We reached the hotel and Alcino screeched to a halt right in front of the entrance. The doorman hurried to open the door. I leaned forward as if I were paying the driver. "We may be up late tonight, Alcino. So maybe you'd better have a siesta."

He nodded.

I got out, noticing that the Italian car had pulled to the curb about fifty yards behind us.

"Didn't I see a men's shop just down the street?" I asked the doorman.

"*Sim.* A very good store, Senhor."

I turned and walked past the small car. I got enough of a look at the driver so I would know him if I saw him again—a round, fat, dark-skinned face with puffed-out cheeks, short black hair, and a black mustache so tiny it was ridiculous. He was careful not to look at me as I went by.

I walked on to the store and entered. I bought a pair of bathing trunks, sandals, beach robe, some underwear and socks, two new shirts, a pair of slacks, and a sports coat. Then I thought of something else.

"What is worn at night when one goes to the clubs around here?"

"Black tie, Senhor. Always. During the summer, which still has two months to go, it is permissible to wear the white coat if one desires."

So I bought a tuxedo with white jacket, shirt and tie, socks, and a pair of black shoes. The clerk added up the total. The prices weren't bad.

"You are staying nearby?" the clerk said.

"Copacabana Palace."

"I shall be happy to have these delivered to you, Senhor, within the hour."

"All right. Let me take the bathing things so I can go down to the beach, and you can deliver the rest of it."

He nodded and wrapped up the trunks, robe, and sandals.

"*Obrigado,* Senhor," he said, handing me the package.

"*Não há de que,*" I said. "Don't mention it."

I went out and headed back for the hotel. The man in the small car was craning his neck to watch the storefront, but as soon as he saw me he quickly turned the other way. I went on past his car and into the hotel. I stopped at the desk.

"Anything for me?" I asked. "March."

"Oh, yes. This came shortly after you left." The clerk took an envelope from back of the desk and handed it to me. It looked like a cablegram. I opened it. It was a check for two thousand dollars. I decided I'd wait until the next morning to cash it.

"Would you put this in the safe for me?" I asked the clerk.

"Certainly, Senhor." He took the envelope and wrote out a receipt for it and pushed it to me. "Have you seen your friend yet?"

I had started to turn away, but that brought me back. "My friend?"

"Yes. He was standing at the desk when this was delivered, and I imagine he saw your name on the envelope. He wanted to know when you had arrived and seemed very pleased to know that you were here. He even called his wife over to tell her that you were here. I thought you might have seen him by this time."

"No," I said. "You haven't mentioned which one of my friends this was."

"Oh—it was Senhor Peter Jackson."

FIVE

When I reached my room, I sat down to think about it. Obviously, Jackson had somehow recognized my name. I thought back over the cases I'd worked on, but I couldn't recall any Peter Jackson. Nor were the other names in the case familiar ones. I was sure that I would have remembered them if they'd been involved in any of my cases. I could think of only one thing. I had always been careful to avoid publicity, but there had been a couple of times I had failed. Jackson must have read about me and knew I was an insurance detective.

I still had one small advantage. I imagined that he didn't know what I looked like, and I did know him by his appearance. If I saw him around the desk, I'd be sure to stay away. If I could keep him from identifying me for a day or two, it might make things easier.

I changed into my swim trunks, tied the robe around me, and put on the sandals. There was a special elevator for people going to the beach. When I got outside in sight of the Italian car, I stopped long enough so the policeman would have a chance to recognize me. The beach was crowded. I walked along, pretending to search for a good spot, looking at everyone I passed. Finally, I spotted them just ahead of me. All three of them were under a beach umbrella. The blonde wore a bikini, and I noticed there was more of her than I had imagined from the photograph.

I walked past them and found a spot not too far away. I slipped out of the robe and sandals and went down to the ocean. I plunged in and swam around for fifteen minutes. It was so pleasant I hated to stop. I walked back up the beach to where I'd left my robe. The three of them were still there. I spread my robe out on the sand and stretched out on it, face down. The sun was hot and I knew I'd better not stay there too long. I put my head down on my arms so I could still see them over the edge of one elbow. But I wasn't near enough to hear what they said.

They seemed to be enjoying themselves. Then, after some conversation, Joseph Sforza stood up. I noticed that while he was short, he wasn't as small as I'd thought he was. He said something, nodding, then started to walk away.

"And bring me an Eskibon," the blonde called, all in English except for the last word. That was Portuguese for Eskimo pie.

"Okay," he called back.

I relaxed beneath the hot sun and felt my eyelids getting heavy. I think I even dozed a little.

Then, suddenly, I heard a muted loudspeaker: "Senhor Milo March. Telephone."

I jumped to my feet, put on the robe, slipped my feet into the sandals, and headed for the hotel. I was halfway there when I cursed to myself. I almost turned back. But the damage, if there was any, was done. I glanced back at the umbrella. Jackson and the blonde seemed engrossed in each other, paying no attention to me. I went ahead to the hotel.

There were several phones for bathers just inside the entrance. I picked up one and told the operator I was Milo March.

"One moment," she said. There was a pause. "Here is your party."

"Hello," I said.

"Hello, sucker," he said in English. There was a click as he hung up.

Well, that took care of that. I went on upstairs, showered, and dressed. I went down to the bar and had two martinis. Then I went into the dining room for lunch.

It was two o'clock by the time I finished. I went out to the lobby. My clothes had been delivered from the store. I took them with me up to my room and put them away. I stepped out on the balcony and looked down to the street. The policeman was still patiently waiting. I stretched out on the bed to take a nap.

It was almost three-thirty when I awakened. I had a fast shower and shave and put on my new slacks and sports coat. I took another look from the balcony. The Italian car was still there. Then I went down and out of the back of the hotel. Alcino was waiting. He smiled as I got in.

"The swim? It was good, Senhor?"

"The swim was good, but that's about all I can say for it. I did see who I'm looking for, but I'm afraid they saw me, too."

"You have never said for whom you look, Senhor. A wife, perhaps? Or a daughter?"

I laughed. "Nothing so romantic, Alcino. I followed two men and a woman who committed crimes in my country. … Do you know where the Copacabana Hill is?"

"Near here."

"I want to stop there for a couple of minutes."

He nodded and started the car. "Are you then of the police, Senhor?" he asked as he pulled out into the street.

"No. I am what we call a private detective in my country. Do you know what that is?"

He nodded vigorously. "Just like the Senhor Bogart in the motion pictures."

"There are a few differences," I said dryly, "but you have the general idea."

"You have many criminals in your country, no?"

"Quite a few, but I doubt if we have more than other countries. You mustn't believe everything you see in motion pictures."

"As you say, Senhor." He pulled into the curb. "Here is the hotel you wished."

"I'll be right back," I said.

I got out and entered the hotel. I looked around until I located the house phones. I went over and picked one up.

"I wish to speak," I said, when the operator had answered, "to Senhor Joseph Sforza, but I have forgotten his room number."

"One moment," she said. Then, "It is room 489. I will ring it for you." I waited and then she was back. "There is no answer, Senhor."

"Muito obrigado," I said.

I replaced the receiver and went back to the taxi.

"It went well, Senhor?" Alcino asked.

"I found out what I wanted. One of the two men is staying here. I only wanted to find out what room he's in."

"And the other man and the woman?"

"They are in the same hotel as I am."

"You are going to arrest them, Senhor?"

"I have no authority to do that. And it wouldn't help if I did have. Your country would not permit them to be taken back."

"I have read about that in the newspapers. There are several Americans here who are wanted in your country. They will be able to stay as long as they have money."

"Lieutenant Alvares?" I asked.

He nodded. "Everyone in Rio knows it. The Lieutenant has a nice big home here and a hacienda in the country. His wife has many servants, and when he is not on duty he drives an American Cadillac."

"I thought as much when I first met him. He must charge high prices for his favors, to live in that style."

Alcino shrugged. "It is said he charges what he can get. From five cruzeiros to a million ... Where to now, Senhor?"

I thought about it a minute. "What time does the night life start in Rio?"

"Perhaps eight or nine."

"Then I think I'll have an early dinner and that will give me plenty of time to get ready for tonight. Any suggestions about a place to go?"

"There are many places. If you would like steak or beef cooked on spits, there is Churrascaria Gaucha."

I shook my head. "I'd rather try some Brazilian food and in some place that doesn't get too many tourists."

"Then you should go to Cabeza Chata. They do have a few tourists, although not too many Americans. The food is good and very reasonable."

"Let's go."

Within a few minutes we stopped near a pleasant-looking building. There was a sign indicating it was Cabeza Chata.

"This is the place, Senhor March," Alcino said.

"Well, let's go."

"But where?" he asked in bewilderment.

"Into the restaurant. I don't know how long we'll be out tonight, and I don't expect you to go without food. So you might as well come in and eat with me. Besides, I'll need some-one to tell me what I should order, and I don't trust waiters."

"But a rich American like you shouldn't share his table with a mere taxi driver …"

"Nonsense. In the first place, I am not rich. The money I'm paying you belongs to the person who is paying me. And I see nothing wrong with having dinner with a taxi driver—unless it keeps you from having dinner with a pretty girl. Come on."

He grinned, and got out of the cab. "You honor me, Senhor."

"No more than you honor me. *Não há de que.*"

We entered the restaurant. It was early, so there were only a sprinkling of people at the tables. Few of them looked like tourists, and all of the customers seemed to be middle class. We took a table in the rear. There was nothing fancy about the tables either, but they were clean and neat. I noticed a block of wood on our table. There were small holes in it. I was going to ask Alcino about it, but the waiter had arrived.

"Boa tarde," he said. He looked at me. *"Donde vem o Senhor?"*

I was surprised at the question, but answered him. "From the United States of America."

He nodded and left.

I looked at Alcino. "What was that all about?"

"You will see," he said.

The waiter was soon back, to place two small flags in the block of wood. One was a Brazilian flag, the other American. I looked around the room and saw there were similar flags on the other occupied tables. Most of them were Brazilian, but I saw two French flags, two Union Jacks, and three representing Germany.

I ordered drinks. Alcino would have nothing but beer and only one at that. He nursed his slowly while I had two. Finally, I was ready to order.

"What should I have, Alcino?" I asked.

"Do you prefer a meat dish or fish?"

"Fish or shellfish, I think."

He nodded and looked up at the waiter. *"Vatapá,"* he said. He considered his own order for a second. *"Picadinhos,"* he added.

The food came and looked delicious. Mine was obviously shrimp in some sort of light-colored sauce. I took a taste and liked it. "What is this?" I asked.

"Shrimp cooked in a sauce of peanuts, palm oil, and coconut milk. Glorious, *não é?"*

I agreed, and lost no more time in conversation. Afterward, we had *fruta de conde,* which turned out to be custard apple, and then *cafèzinho.* The latter is a small cup of coffee, very strong and very hot. It has to cool before you can drink it, but it's about the best coffee you can find anywhere.

We were drinking our coffee when there was a loud, explosive sound from somewhere outside. It was followed by the faint sound of shouts. Alcino did not even look up from his coffee.

"What was that?" I asked.

He shrugged. "Probably a building falling down."

"Only a building falling down? You act as if it happened every day."

"It happens often," he said. "Many buildings are not made well, and after a time they fall down."

"But aren't a lot of people hurt?"

"Very few. There is plenty of warning. Large cracks begin to appear, and the word spreads all over Rio. Everyone who can begins watching each day, and some of them even bet on what day it will fall. Those who live there usually know when the time is near, and they then move. And it provides a sport for many people."

"Some sport," I said.

He smiled. "I have read that in many places there are bird-watchers, but Rio is the only city with building watchers. It is only more proof that there is no city in the world like Rio."

I had to smile back. "On that one point, I have to agree with you."

"It is not only that, Senhor," he said proudly. "Seven or eight years ago, part of a mountain fell on one of our large apartment houses and made it look like a pancake. Can any other city talk of such a feat?"

He had me there. I had to agree that I knew of no other city that could say the same. I called for the check and paid it. It was amazingly small—close to three dollars for both of us. We went out to the taxi.

"Thank you, Senhor," he said as we got into the car.

"*Por qué?*" I asked.

"The dinner. It was not part of our bargain."

"Forget it," I said. "What would I have done without your advice? I would have probably had a terrible meal, and it would have cost me more than the whole check here. Let's go back to the hotel. The rear entrance again."

He drove straight back to the hotel and parked beside the rear entrance. I told him to wait and went upstairs. As soon as I entered my room, I went to the balcony to check on the policeman. He was just coming out of the hotel, scratching his head. I had a hunch he'd gone in to check on me, maybe to call me on the house phone to make sure that I was in.

He reached his car and turned around to look up at the hotel.

I took out a cigarette and lit it, holding the flame as long as I could. He was still staring in my direction when I extinguished the flame and stood there holding the burning cigarette. He continued to stare for a couple of minutes, then got into his car. But he didn't drive away, so he may have recognized me.

I went back into the room and picked up the phone. "Did someone just try to phone me?" I asked the operator when she answered. "This is Milo March."

"Yes, Senhor March. Perhaps two minutes ago. But there was no answer."

"I was unable to reach the phone in time. Is there a message?"

"No. He left no message."

I hung up and went into the bathroom and looked in the mirror. I could use a shave. I stripped off my clothes, shaved and showered, then got dressed in my new evening clothes. Once, before I was fully dressed, I stepped out on the balcony again for a couple of minutes. The Italian car was still there. I went back in and finished dressing.

I turned on the light beside the bed and turned off the overhead light. Then I left the room.

Alcino looked at me as I approached the car, and nodded his head in approval. He reached back and opened the door. "For the grand Senhor."

"Bastante!" I snapped. "Enough. Do you know a nightclub called Jogo do Bicho?"

"Of course, Senhor. We will soon be there."

He started the motor and pulled away.

"Alcino, why is the club called Jogo do Bicho—Animal Game? It hardly sounds like a nightclub."

He chuckled. "You do not know our *jogo do bicho?"*

"What do you mean?"

"It is like a game in many countries—lottery, I think you call it. One can bet whatever one wants to. If one wins, the amount is very large."

"It sounds more like what we call numbers or policy."

"There are no numbers in our game. There are only animals."

"Animals?"

"Yes, Senhor. Once it was a game played only at the zoo. Each day they would put a different animal in a curtained cage. Those who went to the zoo would buy a ticket, which permitted them to guess which animal was in the cage. Those who guessed the right animal won money. It was so successful that someone started it as a game that everyone could play. Now one buys a ticket with the picture of an animal on it. If your animal is picked in the drawing, you win."

"That's very interesting, but it doesn't explain the name of the club."

"Surely, it does, Senhor. A few years ago a man bet everything he had, one thousand cruzeiros, on the lion. Our money was more valuable then. That day only three people in all Rio had bet on a lion. It was drawn, and he was rich. He used the money to open a nightclub, which he named in honor of the game, and now he is richer."

"I'm glad I asked," I said dryly.

"Anytime, Senhor," Alcino said cheerfully. "You are in luck. I know everything about Rio."

"I'll take it in installments, if you don't mind."

"Here we are, Senhor," he said, pulling to the curb. Just ahead of us was a modernistic building with the name of the nightclub spelled out in lights.

"I don't know how long I will be, Alcino," I said. "It depends on what happens inside. I'll have to play it by ear." After I'd said it, I wasn't sure it came off in Portuguese.

"Qué?" he asked in puzzled tones. "I have never heard of a musical instrument that is played with the ear."

"You never heard of an eardrum?" I asked, and left while he was still trying to figure it out.

It was early, so there were not many people in the club. There were five tables occupied by persons who had obviously come to have dinner before the club started filling up. A small orchestra was playing Spanish music. I glanced at the bar. There were two men sitting there, one at each end of the bar. I was about to go on and take a table when the man with his back to me turned his head slightly, and I realized it was Joseph Sforza.

There was a man in front of me. "Table, Senhor?"

"No, thanks," I said. "I think I will sit at the bar for a few minutes."

"As you wish, Senhor."

I walked straight across to the bar and took the stool next to Sforza. The bartender was already in front of me. I glanced over the shelves back of the bar. They seemed to have a variety of imported liquor.

"V.O. and water backed," I said.

I was aware that Sforza looked around when he heard my voice. I heard him suck in his breath with surprise. The bartender brought my drink and took my money. By that time, Sforza must have remembered where he was, for he had recovered.

"Hello, sucker," he said.

"Hi, Joe," I said. I looked at him and there was a cocky smile on his face. "Why didn't you stay on the phone today? We could have had a conversation."

"What about?"

"Maybe about Brazil," I said lightly. "Or just about Rio. There are a lot of interesting things about it. Did you know that it's probably the only city where a mountain fell on an apartment house? Or that there is no extradition treaty between Brazil and the United States?"

He snickered. "I know that."

"But did you also know that it has a cop who is very inter-ested in the people who come here because there is no extra-dition?"

"What are you talking about?" he asked.

"I thought it was clear. There is a cop around who concerns himself with the welfare of people who come here because there is no extradition. The only catch is that the cop usually ends up with all the money."

I signaled the bartender for another drink. Sforza waited until I was served and had paid.

"Who's this cop?" he asked then.

I shook my head. "If you haven't met him, you will. Why should I spoil your little surprises? But you may remember that last year two men voluntarily returned to the States. One of them went back before his money was gone. The other one ran out of money and tried to make more here. Then he went back rather than face a Brazilian court. Keep it in mind."

"Nuts," he said. He looked at me, frowning. "What are you trying to say?"

"Nothing," I said. "I'm just making a small suggestion. If you and Jackson took your money and returned to America, the fact that you returned most of the money would probably help your case."

"Nuts," he said again. He turned to face me more squarely. "Look, sucker, we know all about you. You ain't even a regu-lar cop. You're just a lousy insurance dick. You ain't got noth-ing to say down here, so just get off our backs. If you want to be smart, you'll go back yourself and mark the whole thing off as a vacation."

"Maybe," I said easily.

"We're just tourists down here having a good time," he said. "We ain't doing anything that a cop can shake us down for. You nose around too much and we'll go to the cops about you."

I laughed. "How did you know who I am?"

He considered it for a minute, then finally decided he had nothing to lose by answering. "Pete read a story about you once. It said that several insurance companies gave you their big cases."

"What case was it about?"

"Where some guys burned down a house in Los Angeles."*

"Then Pete must not have read the small print," I said, "or he would also have found out that several pretty tough guys died in the process."

He glanced at my coat. "You ain't even heeled. And down here you wouldn't dare."

"Okay, Joe," I said. I finished my drink. "But you ought to think it over. If you could also take the credit for making Jackson go back, you might get off very lightly. Jackson probably did all the trigger-pulling anyway. And you may be next on his list. Every time he pulled the trigger, it meant a bigger share. Why should he stop now? Well, good luck—sucker."

I slid off the stool and left before he could answer. I went back and got a table toward the rear of the room so that I could see most of it. I ordered a drink and watched as people began straggling into the club. Joseph Sforza was still sitting at the bar, scowling into his drink.

---

* See *Softly in the Night* by M.E. Chaber.

It was about thirty minutes later when Jackson and the girl came in. She was wearing an evening dress that made her look almost as good as the bikini had. The headwaiter saw them and led them over to a table near the bandstand. Sforza saw them and hurried over. They gave an order to the waiter, and as soon as he left, Sforza started talking to them, leaning across the table. They were all very careful not to look in my direction, but I had no doubt that he was telling them about his conversation with me.

Their conversation continued animatedly for some time, interrupted only by the appearance of the waiter with their drinks. Later they ordered more drinks, but the conversation had stopped, except for occasional exchanges. They still ignored me.

A singer came out and worked with the band for a few numbers. She was a tall, chesty brunette with a pretty good voice, who sang in Spanish and Portuguese. By this time the club was well filled. The singer left the stand, and couples began to dance. Jackson got up to dance with the girl, but I noticed they were careful to stay away from the section where I sat.

A short, dark man stopped beside my table. He looked down at me. *"Fala o Senhor portugues?"* he asked.

I admitted that I spoke some Portuguese.

He waved the waiter over to the table. "Give the gentleman a drink," he said. He turned back to me. "Permit me to introduce myself, Senhor. I am José Eiríco Fonesca. I am the owner of this place. I believe that this is your first visit to our club, no?"

"Yes," I said.

The waiter arrived with my free drink.

"Welcome to Jogo do Bicho," the owner said. "If you are interested, we also serve quite good food, both American and Portuguese. Later, there will be two complete floor shows—with very pretty girls. I trust you will visit us again."

"Thank you," I said. I looked at him with interest. "So you're the man who won enough on a lion to start a night-club?"

He smiled. "So you know that story? You must have spent some time in Rio."

"No. My taxi driver told me about it on the way over when I remarked that it was a strange name for a club." I glanced across the room. Jackson and the blonde had gone back to their table.

He must have followed my glance, or he had noticed me watching them before.

"The blonde is very pretty," he said, "but I have never seen her speak to anyone except her husband or their friend. They are very strange people."

"How is that?" I asked.

"They have been coming here almost every night for a week, but I do not think they enjoy themselves. I get many tourists here, and they all enjoy Rio and they enjoy my club. But I sometimes feel that those come here because they have no other place to go and that to them Rio is just another city. It is too bad." He shook his head in sympathy. "Did I not see you speaking with their friend at the bar earlier?"

"Casual talk at a bar," I said. "But I think you're right about them. I told their friend that Rio was the only city where a mountain ever fell on an apartment house, but he didn't seem to be interested."

"That is what I mean," he said, nodding. "But you, Senhor, I can see are different. You do not act like a tourist, more like a businessman perhaps. But you still enjoy yourself."

"I try to," I said. I lifted the last drink the waiter had brought. "To your good health, Senhor Fonesca."

"Thank you," he said gravely.

Then he was gone, quietly threading his way among the tables as he surveyed his little kingdom.

When I looked across the room again, Sforza, Jackson, and Betty Bell were leaving the club. I smiled and let them go. I had apparently succeeded in making them nervous, which was all I had hoped to accomplish this soon.

I sat for another half hour, having another drink, then called for my check. I paid it and walked outside. I looked around and saw that Alcino was parked in the same spot. I walked down to the car and bent slightly to open the door.

There was a shot. Something screeched off the top of the taxi and screamed off into the distance.

SIX

I threw open the door and jumped in the car, getting down out of sight. Glancing up front, I saw that Alcino had prudently done the same.

"Should I drive away quickly, Senhor?" he asked.

"No," I said. "I don't think he will, but he might shoot again if he can see anyone. I don't believe he'll risk coming up to the car."

I reached over and rolled down the window. A moment later I heard the distant sound of running footsteps. Then, from more than a block away, a motor started up and faded into the distance.

"All right, Alcino," I said, sitting up. "I think we can move now."

He straightened up and his white teeth flashed in a smile as he looked back at me. "Someone shoots at the Senhor, no?"

"I got that general idea."

"You should shoot back at him, Senhor. I know where there is a gun that can be bought."

"I've got a gun," I said shortly. "All I need is the right to use it. Maybe tomorrow … In the meantime, let's go back to the hotel."

"So early?"

"Yes. I've accomplished the first thing. I've made them

nervous. Tomorrow will be soon enough to put on a little more pressure."

He started the motor and drove off. "To the rear entrance as usual, Senhor?" he asked.

"No," I said. "Let's go to the front entrance. The policeman may still be there, waiting for the light to go out in my room. If he is, it ought to shake him up a little to see me coming in."

Alcino chuckled. He seemed to be in favor of anything that would shake up the police, proving that cab drivers are pretty much the same the world over.

He pulled up in front of the hotel with a flourish. The doorman came to open the door. I took out four dollars and handed them to Alcino.

"Better come early in the morning," I said. "About nine o'clock."

"I will be here," he said. "Which entrance, Senhor?"

"Right here," I said.

I got out and stood there for a minute, looking around. The Italian car was still in the same place, and I could dimly see the driver leaning forward to stare through his windshield. Then he started his motor and the little car moved out into the street, the motor snarling angrily from the accelerator having been pushed too hard. I smiled and went inside.

I stopped at the desk, but there was nothing for me. I picked up a newspaper and some cigarettes in the lobby and then stopped in at the bar for a last drink. The bar was doing a brisk business, although it was not crowded. I ordered a drink and sipped it slowly, looking around the room. There were a couple of pretty women, but both were with their husbands—or reasonable facsimiles. I finished my drink and went upstairs.

I undressed, turned on some music, and got into bed with the newspaper. By the time I'd finished reading it, I was getting sleepy. I picked up the phone and left a call for eight o'clock, then turned off the light.

The phone awakened me the next morning. I thanked the operator and had her connect me with room service. I stayed in bed until my breakfast arrived. After I'd eaten, I went in and examined my face in the mirror. I decided I didn't have to shave until later in the day. I had a quick shower and went downstairs. I stopped at the desk and picked up my check.

Alcino was waiting when I went outside. I climbed in the taxi and told him to take me to the nearest bank. I watched as we pulled away, but there wasn't anyone following us that I could spot.

At the bank, I identified myself and cashed the check. I had them give it to me in dollars. I went back to the taxi.

"Now," I told Alcino, "I want to visit our friend Lieutenant Alvares again."

He nodded and we were off, dodging through traffic and missing cars and pedestrians by inches. I tried to be philosophical about it and keep my thoughts on a higher plane, but it was difficult. I was glad when we arrived at police headquarters.

I went in and stopped at the desk inside the door. "Lieutenant Alvares," I said. "My name is Milo March."

The desk man nodded and picked up his phone, pushing a

button. "Senhor Milo March to see the Lieutenant," he said. He listened, then hung up. "He will see you, Senhor."

I nodded and went up the stairs. I knocked on the door of the Lieutenant's office.

"*Entra,*" he called.

I opened the door and went in.

He looked up, a faint smile on his face. "Ah, Senhor March," he said. "Sit down."

I took the same chair I had occupied the day before. "*Como está?*" I asked politely.

"Very well," he said. "You are enjoying your stay in Rio, Senhor?"

"Very much," I said.

One of my policemen tells me that you fooled him last night."

"That is true."

"I suppose you left by the rear of the hotel and kept a light burning in your room. He should have thought of that. But it is difficult to get policemen with imaginations. Why did you do it, Senhor March?"

"I don't like to be followed," I said bluntly. "You must have assigned a more imaginative man. I haven't spotted one yet this morning."

"You are not being followed this morning. Yesterday, all I knew about you was from the documents you presented. As you know, documents can be purchased. But I took advantage of your suggestion and sent a cable to Lieutenant Rockland in New York City." He picked up a cablegram on his desk and put it in front of me. "You might be interested in seeing his answer."

I looked down at it. I had to smile as I read.

MILO MARCH IS A DULY LICENSED PRIVATE DETECTIVE IN NEW
YORK AND OTHER STATES. HE IS EXTREMELY OPINIONATED AND
STUBBORN BUT HAS AN IRRITATING WAY OF OFTEN BEING RIGHT.
IF HE BREAKS ANY LAWS HE MUST DO IT DISCREETLY FOR WE HAVE
NEVER CAUGHT HIM AT IT. I CONSIDER HIM TO BE COMPLETELY
RELIABLE. GIVE HIM MY REGARDS.

LT. JOHN ROCKLAND

"Lieutenant Rockland never could send a short telegram," I
said. "I'm glad you asked him about me. I came in to suggest
that you do so."

"Why?"

"Somebody shot at me last night."

"Where?"

"Just outside Jogo do Bicho."

"Ah," he said, "then you have an idea who did it."

"An idea, but that's all. I didn't see anyone."

"If you'd like to make a complaint, I can do something
about it."

"No complaint," I said. "I didn't see anyone and I can't
swear to anything."

"If you hadn't fooled my man last night, he might have
caught the one who shot at you." He sighed as if the weight
of the world were on his shoulders. "What did you want,
Senhor March?"

"It may happen again," I said. "I'd like to be able to protect
myself."

"Meaning?"

"Meaning that I'd like to get a temporary permit to carry a gun for the remainder of my stay in Rio."

There was a slight change in the expression of his face. I recognized the look, and I felt sure I'd get the permit.

"That is a big request, Senhor," he said. "Even with the kind words of the American police lieutenant. I do not know how you do these things in your country, but we do not make it so easy for just anyone to carry guns here."

"Sure, it's a big request. And you're a big man, Lieutenant."

"What does that mean, Senhor?"

"It means, what do you have to lose? I have respectable references, so the police department can in all good conscience give me a permit. If I misuse it, you can always arrest me. On the other hand, if I can protect myself and survive, I might be even more useful to you."

"How?"

I leaned across the desk. "Let us be honest with each other, Lieutenant Alvares, even if it's only for a moment. You think you smell money about the three people I followed here. You've smelled out a lot of money before. But this time you can't find it. You think that I might lead you to it. This brings up two possibilities. If they should kill me while I'm acting as a bird dog for you, you might be able to arrest them and then find the money. But if that fails, you no longer have a bird dog. So it might be better to keep me alive so that I can lead you to the money you think you smell. Then, once you have it, you can kill me—or try to—and nobody else will dare testify against you."

He stared at me and for just a second the film dropped from his eyes and there was nothing there but greed and death. Then the film lifted again and he smiled at me.

"I sometimes think," he said, "that you *norte-americanos* see too many motion pictures. But you are right about one thing. You do have good references. There is still, however, a matter of laws to comply with."

"Of course," I said. "I did not ask you to ignore them. What are they?"

"Do you have a gun?"

"I can always get one," I answered, ignoring the direct question.

"Where?"

"A dozen places. You must know that as well as I do."

He nodded, smiling. "But it must be a gun that can be registered, you understand. If it should turn out to be a gun that has been stolen, you will be in serious trouble."

"I understand that," I said. "What else?"

"You will have to put up a bond. This will be returned to you on the expiration of your permit, if you have not violated any of our laws. The permit will have to be renewed at the end of a week."

"How much is the bond?"

"One hundred and eighty thousand cruzeiros."

That was about three hundred dollars, cheaper than I had thought it would be.

"And where is that paid?"

"Downstairs. Room 101. But you do not pay the bond until the license form has been filled out."

"And there is a fee for that?"

"Naturally. Did you not pay a fee when you secured a license in your own country?"

"Yes. How much is the fee for the license?"

"Five hundred dollars—in American dollars."

I knew the answer to the next question, but I asked it anyway. "And where is that paid?"

"In this office," he said. He opened a drawer in his desk and pulled out a pad of forms. "You wish the temporary license, Senhor?"

"Yes," I said. I took some money from my pocket, holding it low enough so that he couldn't see it, and separated five one-hundred-dollar bills. I put them on the desk, but nearer to me than to him.

He smiled and picked up a pen. "Your full name is Milo March?"

"Yes."

He wrote it down. "And your Rio address is the Copacabana Palace Hotel?"

"Yes," I said again.

He continued to ask questions—age, height, weight, color of hair and eyes, and other questions of general information—writing my replies down as I answered. Then he pushed the form and the pen across to me. "If you will sign at the bottom, Senhor March ..."

I signed. As I finished, he reached out and took the five hundred dollars. He didn't bother to play any games. He merely folded them and put them in his pocket.

"You will now take that to Room 101," he said. "They will

take a photograph of you and paste it on the form. They will also put your right thumbprint on it. You will give them the permit and they will stamp it, so that it will show that you have deposited the bond."

"It will then be good?"

He shook his head. "When you have acquired a gun, you must bring it to the same room. They will check the serial number against those of stolen guns. If it is not there, they will make a record of the serial number and also place it on the license. It will then be in force."

"No other payments?" I asked.

"No other payments," he said.

"If the permit is not in force, how do I get the gun here in order to have the serial number placed on it?"

"If you will look on the back of the license, you will notice that it says the bearer is permitted to transport a gun from the spot where he gets possession of it to the police headquarters. You are a cautious man, Senhor March."

"It's one way to stay alive," I said. I stood up. *"Obrigado,* Lieutenant Alvares."

"Não há de que," he said. He gave me another one of those mirthless smiles. "It is a pleasure to help our friends from the north."

"I know," I said, thinking of the five hundred dollars I'd given him.

I left and went downstairs to Room 101. Things happened just the way he had said they would. I was photographed and the small picture was pasted on the form.

They rolled my right thumb on an inkpad and pressed it to

another part of the paper. They took my money and stamped the form and gave me a receipt for the money. They repeated the fact that I would have to bring the gun in so they could check the serial number. I thanked them and that was all there was to it.

"You were gone a long time," Alcino said when I got into the taxi. "I was worried."

"There was nothing to worry about—except my money," I said. "Let's go back to the hotel."

"The front?"

"Yes."

We drove straight back, without spotting a tail, and Alcino parked near the entrance. I told him I'd be right down. I went upstairs, put on the shoulder holster, and slipped my gun into it. I put an extra box of shells in my coat pocket and went downstairs again.

"Back to the police," I told him.

Alcino gave a mock groan but made a fast U-turn and headed back the way we'd come. He parked in the same spot we'd been in before.

"This time I will not be so long," I told him as I got out. I entered the building and went straight to Room 101. They took my gun and trotted off to check it with their files. That took about fifteen minutes, and then the man returned to say that the gun was all right.

"This is a very good gun," he commented as he entered the serial number on my permit. "Where did the Senhor buy it?"

"From a man," I said.

He shook his head. "The Senhor is fortunate. Many such

guns turn out to be ones that have been stolen." He finished writing, slammed another stamp on the permit, and pushed it and the gun toward me. "There you are, Senhor."

"Obrigado," I said.

I slipped the gun into the holster and the permit into my wallet. I went back to the taxi. As soon as I was in the back seat, I opened my coat.

"You see," I told Alcino, "I can protect myself after this."

"Legally?" he asked.

"Completely."

"It did not come cheaply," he observed.

"No, the Lieutenant is taking care of his old-age security. But it might have been higher if he didn't think I might lead him to what he wants."

"Money?"

I nodded.

"It is here in Rio?"

"I think so and he thinks so, but neither one of us is sure."

"Ah, that one has a nose for money," he said. "Where to, Senhor?"

I looked at my watch. It was almost eleven o'clock. "Let's take a chance. The Copacabana Hill Hotel."

He nodded and we were off.

When we reached the hotel, I went directly to the desk. "Has Senhor Sforza left the hotel yet?"

"I think not," the clerk said. "I believe that the Senhor is having breakfast in the serving area of the bar. Shall I have him paged for you?"

"Don't bother," I said. "I'll go in and surprise him. Thank you."

I went into the bar and looked around. They had a section divided from the bar itself by a two-thirds wall with open panels. Sforza was sitting by himself, eating.

I stopped at the bar. "I'm joining that gentleman over there," I said indicating Sforza. "Will you send over a dry martini for me? You can put it on his bill."

"Certainly, Senhor," the bartender said.

I went in and took the chair across from Sforza. "Good morning," I said brightly. "I hope you don't mind if I join you?"

"Why don't you get lost?" he growled.

"I have the unerring instinct of a homing pigeon," I said. "Who was the lousy shot last night? You or Jackson?"

"I don't know what you're talking about," he grunted. "I just don't like sitting with a cop."

"But you pointed out last night that I'm not a cop."

"Anyway, you're spoiling my breakfast."

"Oh, well," I said, "it's still better than the food you'd get in a Brazilian prison."

"Drop it," he said.

The waiter arrived with my martini. He put it in front of me and departed.

"What the hell do you want?" Sforza asked.

I took a sip. It was a good martini. "I don't want anything, Joe. What do you want? Especially from your partner, Jackson. What did Myers, Dallin, and Petrie want?"

"You're nuts," he said. He was looking at my coat. "I see you collected some hardware."

"After last night, I decided I needed it."

"Do the local cops know?"

"They know," I said cheerfully. "I have a permit."

"Like I said, beat it. I don't like cops or guys who are chummy with cops."

"Did you think about what I said last night?"

"I didn't pay any attention to anything you said. Why should I?"

"Who knows? The life you save may be your own."

"You don't know what you're talking about," he said, but his voice lacked conviction. "Pete and me have been pals for a long time."

"The other guys were his pals, too. Did you tell Jackson about our conversation when he came into the club last night?"

"Why?"

"It was a mistake, Joe. He'll start thinking that you might listen to me, and one of these days he'll look at you through the sights of that .38."

"To hell with you," Sforza said roughly.

"He probably talked you into taking that shot at me last night," I said. "If you'd shot straighter, he'd have seen to it that the Rio cops found out about it. Then there would be a whole million dollars for just him and Betty."

"I don't know nothing about no million dollars." His voice was getting a little hoarse.

I finished my drink. "All right, Joe. But you'd better think about it some more before it's too late. You can't win when you're in between your pal and a hungry cop." I stood up. "I'll see you around, Joe. Thanks for the martini."

I went back to the taxi.

"He was there?" Alcino asked.

"He was there. I pushed him a little more."

"The one who shot at you last night?"

"I think so. Now, Alcino, I want to exchange some dollars for cruzeiros."

He nodded and we drove off. We drove through various strange streets for about ten or fifteen minutes and finally came to a stop in what seemed to be a lower-middle-class neighborhood.

"I will be but a minute, Senhor," Alcino said. He jumped out and went into what I took to be a beer and wine tavern. He was gone about three minutes. When he returned, he put his head inside the cab. "He will give you eleven hundred cruzeiros for each dollar, but he can't take more than five hundred dollars at the moment. If you want more, we should come back later."

"Five hundred will be enough," I said. I took five hundred dollars from my pocket and handed it to Alcino.

"You want me to exchange it?" he asked in surprise.

"Surely. Why not?"

"But you do not know me, Senhor. I might cheat you."

"I know you, Alcino, and I don't think you'd cheat me."

"Thank you, Senhor." He went back into the building. When he returned, he handed me a large bundle of notes. I stuck them in my pocket without counting them.

"Where to, Senhor?" Alcino asked, slipping behind the wheel.

"I think we'll go back to the hotel," I said. "You can take

the rest of the afternoon off. I don't think I can do much until tonight. You can even pick me up late, maybe around eight o'clock. I'll try to catch our friends at the nightclubs again."

He nodded and didn't say anything until we reached the hotel.

"Senhor," he said then, twisting around in the seat, "what will you do for dinner if I pick you up so late?"

"I don't know," I said. "I'll eat either here at the hotel or when I reach the club."

"Have you ever been to the *favelas*, Senhor?"

"No," I said.

I was puzzled. I knew what he was talking about, but not why. The *favelas* were the shacks that made up Rio de Janeiro's slum area. I knew that the poorest people in Rio lived there and that the shanties in some cases existed on some of the most valuable land in Rio. That was about the extent of my knowledge.

"Would you like to see what it is like there, Senhor?"

"Sure. Maybe we can go after this is over."

"No," he said almost stubbornly. "I meant this evening, before you go to the clubs."

"What do you have in mind, Alcino?" I asked.

"My wife," he said, not looking at me. "I told her about you insisting that I eat with you yesterday. She said that I should bring you to dinner tonight. I said no, that you would not enjoy coming to the *favelas*, and she said that you did not sound like such a man to her. She also pointed out that today is a saint's day and that we should have a special meal anyway. Then my two sons got into it also, insisting that they had never met a *norteamericano*, and my wife added that I was depriving them. You know how women are, Senhor. I had to mention it to you or I would have had no peace at home for a month."

I smiled. "Your wife is right, Alcino. I will be very happy to come to your home for the evening meal. How old are your two boys?"

His face was alight with a broad smile. "Five and seven, Senhor. And you have saved my life. You are sure you do not mind, Senhor?"

"Quite the contrary," I said. "I'll be delighted. What time will you pick me up?"

"I thought at five o'clock, which will get us back in plenty of time for you to go to the clubs." Then he added, as though to reassure me, "My wife is a very good cook."

"I'm sure she is," I said.

I got out and went into the hotel. I stopped at the desk. There was no mail, but the clerk said I'd had two phone calls. It had been a man each time, but he had not left a name. He had merely said he would call again.

"Have you yet become reunited with your friend, Senhor Jackson?" he asked.

"Oh, we're closer than ever," I said. "If I get another call, I'll be having lunch."

I went in and sat at the bar for my first martini. I had the second one sent to a table and I ordered some lunch. They hadn't brought it yet when the waiter came and told me there was a phone call for me and that I could take it on one of the house phones in the bar. I walked in and picked up the phone. The operator connected me.

"This," said a man's voice in English, "is Fred Bruce. You don't know me, but we have a mutual friend in New York named Rockland. I'd like to talk to you whenever it's convenient."

"Where are you?" I asked.

"In my room here in the hotel."

"I'm just about to have lunch. Come on down and join me. I'm in the small dining room just off the bar. Do you know what I look like?"

"No."

"Well, I'm wearing a brown and white sports coat. I think I'm the only person sitting alone in the room. And I'll have a martini in front of me."

"I'll be right down."

I went back to my table and told the waiter to hold my lunch a few minutes, but to bring me another martini. I already had it when I saw a young man enter and look around. He was probably in his middle twenties, built like a football player. He was wearing sports clothes, but there was something about him that suggested he was a cop. He spotted me and came across.

"Milo March?" he asked.

I nodded. "Sit down."

He took the chair across from me and pulled out his wallet. He flipped it open and held it out to me. "This is my identification."

I glanced at it. It said that Frederic Bruce was a Sergeant, Detective Division, New York City Police Department.

"Put it away," I said, "before somebody else sees it. You

look enough like a cop without advertising it to everybody. Johnny sent you?"

"Yes, sir."

"Don't call me sir. It makes me feel too damn ancient. Call me Milo. I should have known better than to give that bastard as a reference so he'd know where I was."

He laughed. "That's what the Lieutenant said you'd say."

"He did, did he? What do you want to drink?"

"Nothing," he said, but he hesitated a minute before saying it.

"No drinking on duty and all that jazz? Forget it. In the first place, you may not even get a chance to be on duty. And nobody comes to Rio without having a few drinks. You'll stand out like a sore thumb. Now, what will you have?"

"A manhattan."

I beckoned the waiter and told him what to bring. "Had lunch yet?"

"No. I wanted to get in touch with you and I was afraid I might miss you."

"I've already ordered. See what you want." I handed him the menu.

The waiter came back and he ordered his lunch. I told the waiter to bring mine and his together.

"Now," I said, when the waiter was gone, "what the hell was the idea of Johnny Rockland sending you down here?"

"All I know is what the Lieutenant said. He told me that you were after the men who pulled the armored truck robbery upstate and also killed one of their own men in the city. He said he'd bet a month's salary you'd find them, and another month's salary that you'd find some way to get them back to the States. He said the State Police weren't paying any attention to you, and that if you got the men back, there ought to be someone on hand to arrest them. And he said I might come in handy if you needed my help."

"I'll have a few words with him about that when I get back. Anything else?"

He smiled. "Yes, he gave me quite a lecture. He told me not to be fooled by the fact you're a private detective; that you're as good as any cop. He said I wasn't to try to do anything on my own but to do only what you told me. And he added that I wasn't to tell you what he said."

The waiter brought our food. He served it and left.

"I hope," I said, "you didn't declare your profession when you entered the country."

"No."

"And didn't try to bring in any guns, badges, or cuffs?"

"No. But I see you're carrying a gun. Aren't you afraid they'll pick you up for that?"

"I have a permit."

He looked surprised. "How did you manage that?"

"A crooked cop who hopes I'm going to lead him to a million dollars, the payment of a three hundred dollar bond plus a five hundred dollar bribe to the same crooked cop, and the fact that someone took a shot at me last night. It was simple."

"Who tried to shoot you? One of the three?"

"I think so, but I can't prove it."

"You have located them?"

"Oh, yes. That's the easiest part of it. Jackson and the girl are staying in this hotel. Sforza is in a hotel about three blocks from here."

"How did they get the money into the country?"

"That," I said, "is something that a Lieutenant Alvares and I both would like to know—as well as where it is now."

We had finished our lunch and were almost through with our coffee.

"What do we do now?" Bruce asked.

I smiled. "Did you bring your swim trunks?"

He looked puzzled. "No. Why?"

"Go buy a pair while I'm taking care of the check. We're going swimming. I'll meet you at the bathers' exit downstairs."

He still looked puzzled, but he got up and left. I paid the bill and went upstairs. I got out of my clothes and put on my trunks. I took a look at my back in the mirror. It was a little red from the day before. I put on my robe and sandals and went downstairs. I had to wait about five minutes before Fred Bruce showed up.

When we reached the beach, I stopped and rented an umbrella. The sun was hot and I didn't want too much of it. We started walking along the beach.

"There's a good spot," Fred said, pointing. It was a fairly empty space, but I noticed it wasn't far from a group of pretty girls.

"Sorry," I said, "I have another spot in mind."

We walked about three hundred yards before I spotted them. I led the way to an area not more than twenty feet from the three of them. I put up the umbrella and took off my robe. Then I pretended to catch sight of them suddenly.

"Come on, Fred," I said. "I want you to meet someone."

He looked surprised, but followed me across the sand. They had already seen me, and they watched our approach with blank expressions.

"Hi," I said cheerfully as we reached them. I looked at Jackson. "Pete, as an old friend who was so delighted to find out I was here, I thought you'd like to meet another old friend I just ran into. Joseph Sforza, Peter Jackson, Betty Bel—sorry, I mean Betty Jackson, I'd like you to meet my friend, Fred Bruce."

Fred was taken by surprise, but he managed to say hello. Jackson and Sforza managed surly grunts. The girl didn't say anything; she just looked at the two of us.

"Fred," I said, "is a Sergeant in the New York City Police Department—here on vacation, of course."

There was a moment of silence. "Geez," Sforza finally said to nobody in particular, "I thought this was supposed to be a high-class beach, but it's lousy with cops."

"Beat it, March," Jackson said. His voice sounded tight with anger. "And take your cop friend with you. You ain't got no authority here and we ain't done nothing, so leave us alone. We got a right to privacy."

"Oh, you'll get that later," I said cheerfully. "We have very private rooms reserved for all of you back in the States." I looked at the girl. "You want us to go, too, honey?"

"Yes," she said.

"You ought to try a more friendly approach," I said. "After

all, we're going to be closer than kissing cousins until we all get back to the States. Come on, Fred."

I turned and took a couple of steps away from them. Then I turned to look back.

"By the way, Joe, did I remember to thank you for that martini at your hotel? I hope so. And remember what I told you."

SEVEN

We walked back to our umbrella. I kicked off my sandals and led the way to the ocean before Fred could start asking questions. We plunged into the water and swam for several minutes. Finally, I left the water and headed back to the beach. As I trudged up the sand, it looked as if Jackson and Sforza were quarreling. But as they caught sight of me, they stopped. I went to sit under our umbrella.

Fred stayed in the water for another few minutes, then ran up to join me.

"Hey, that's great water," he said as he sat down.

"It's a great place," I said. "Beautiful city, beautiful women, excellent food—what more can you ask for?"

"Maybe I'm in the wrong end of the business," he said with a smile. "Is this the way you always work?"

"When I can. Know a better way?"

"What was that business before? I thought you didn't want anyone to know I'm a cop?"

"They don't count," I said, nodding toward the three. "It's the rest of the town that I don't want to know about it, especially the local police."

"I still don't get what the introduction was about."

I got a cigarette out of my robe and lit it. "Did Johnny tell you anything about how I work?"

"No. He merely said that you get results."

"I don't have some of the advantages of the police," I said. "I don't have a force of experts to rely on. I can't use search warrants. If I want to arrest someone, I can only make a citizen's arrest. I can't drag anyone in and question them until they break. All of those things are denied private detectives."

"Of course," he said. "It wouldn't do if everyone had those rights."

"I agree," I said. "It's bad enough that the police have them. But you see I have a problem all the time, which for the first time you are facing to some degree."

"Me? I don't understand."

"Your reason for being down here, Fred, is pretty much the same as mine: to see Peter Jackson, Joseph Sforza, and Betty Bell back in the United States to be tried for grand larceny and murder. The only difference is that you'd like to see the money returned, while I *must* see it returned. Otherwise, for once we are completely equal."

"Not quite. You have a gun and I don't."

"That advantage is only in connection with saving my own life, and I'm not sure how much it's worth there—except psychologically. Now, then, remembering that we are in a country which has no extradition treaty with our country, and a country in which you are nothing but a tourist, what would you do? How would you go about accomplishing the goal we agree we both want to achieve?"

"Well," he said uncertainly, "I'm not sure that I can give an answer this quickly. I presume I would first try to get the cooperation of the local police."

"Johnny should have explained something else to you," I said gently. "It doesn't exist. American law enforcement officers have long experience with this problem. I might also point out that this case is further complicated by the presence of a police lieutenant with a nose for money—and hands, as well. If he could get possession of that million dollars, he would probably drive the three people happily out of the country into our arms. Do you have any other plan of action?"

He rubbed his chin. "I guess it wouldn't do any good to try to talk to them with the murder raps hanging over them," he admitted. "I suppose I might try to trick them into leaving the country."

"Not very good, Fred. It would be hard enough to trick Jackson or Sforza into leaving Brazil. But you can also be sure that Lieutenant Alvares knows every move that those three make. So if you could trick them into something, you could be sure that the good Lieutenant would be on hand."

He threw up his hands. "All right. I give up. I don't know what to do. What does this have to do with telling them I'm from the New York police?"

"Since I'm denied the methods I mentioned earlier, when I'm sure that I know the guilty persons, I start pushing them. Sooner or later it causes panic. Once that hits them, they're going to start making mistakes. The more mistakes they make, the more vulnerable they are. I started pushing Sforza yesterday. I pushed him some more this morning. And a few minutes ago. And now they know about you, and they'll never be sure that you aren't around somewhere even if they see me alone."

"You think it'll work?"

"It already has. They tried to shoot me last night. Today Sforza knows that I have a gun, and just now he found out that you're around. In the meantime, Jackson knows that I've been suggesting to Sforza that he cooperate with me. The two of them were quarreling when I came out of the water a few minutes ago. They stopped when they saw me."

"It might work at that," he said. "What do you think will happen?"

I shrugged. "A lot of things can happen. I've also suggested to Sforza that he might be next on the list to get a bullet from his pal Jackson. So he might decide to cooperate."

"You mean you think he'll cooperate in getting the other two to leave?"

"No," I said in disgust. "The first thing is to find the money. Then I'll worry about getting them out of here—and that will be the easier part. Of course, it's always possible that Jackson will get rid of Sforza before we can use him. However, we might be able to do something with that, too. And don't forget there's one additional factor in our charming little game."

"What's that?"

"A very amiable cop waiting in the wings to pick up the chips." I looked at my watch. "Well, I'm going in."

"Where are you going?"

"I have a dinner date with a taxi driver."

"But when are we going to work?"

"We already have worked," I said. "Why don't you see if you can get acquainted with one of the lovely chicks here and relax? It'll be good for your blood pressure."

"Wait," he said as I started off. "When will I see you?"

"Tonight or tomorrow," I said, and kept on going. As I walked past the other umbrella, I winked at the blonde.

I went up to my room and got dressed. It was early, but I went downstairs. There were some shops in the hotel and I picked up toys for two boys of five and seven. After some thought about it, I bought a pretty shawl for Alcino's wife. Then I went into the bar and had a couple of drinks. I doubted if Alcino would serve any cocktails.

When it was almost five o'clock I went outside to wait. I glanced across at the beach and saw Fred Bruce standing up and talking to an attractive dark-haired girl. As I watched, they turned and raced to the ocean. I guessed that I wouldn't have to worry about him for the rest of the evening. I was brought back to the present by the sound of a horn. Alcino was at the curb. I went over and got into the cab.

"What are the packages, Senhor?" he asked.

"Some bargains I ran into. I didn't have time to take them up to the room. I hope you don't mind?"

"But no, Senhor." He made a U-turn and headed back toward the city.

We drove steadily, and in several minutes I could see that we were coming to the poorer section of town. Soon we were in it. The shacks were clustered on either side so thickly that it would have been difficult to put a hand between two houses without touching them both. The street was filled with goats and chickens and shouting kids. Alcino drove slowly through them, and finally stopped in front of one of the shacks. It looked exactly like the others.

"This is a poor neighborhood, Senhor," he said. "Many of the people here do not make as much money in a week as I make in one day. But they manage to live, and if you were to come here often, you would find they are the happiest people in Rio."

"But you surely make enough money to move to a larger house, one where there would be a yard for your children, where your wife wouldn't have to work so hard."

"And what would I do there, Senhor? All of my friends are here. All of my children's friends are here. And my wife's. Here, I can even lie in bed and talk with my neighbor, who is also lying in bed. Could I do that in such a house as you mention? And, living here, I can save money so that my children can go to fine schools, and it has still permitted me to buy many things for my wife which make her life easier. You will see. Come with me, Senhor. Bring your packages so that the children will not be tempted."

"I intended to," I said.

I gathered up my packages and got out of the taxi. The children in the street looked at me with curiosity as I followed Alcino into the house.

It consisted of three small rooms, but they were neat, and I noticed that the furniture was better than the outside of the house would indicate. Then a woman and two wide-eyed little boys were in front of me, obviously dressed in their finest, and Alcino was introducing me to his wife. She was a pretty little dark-haired woman with a merry face.

"Senhor March," she said, "you honor our house by coming here."

"I feel that I am the one who is honored," I said.

"And here," Alcino said proudly, "are Getulio and Manuel."

The two children shyly shook hands, their faces solemn.

Alcino then led the way into the living room. A table had been set up in the center of it. It was covered with a lace table-cloth and there were candles in the center.

"I have explained to my wife," Alcino said, "that we must work tonight, so she will serve us at once if that is all right with you."

"Fine," I said, "but first I must get rid of these packages."

I handed one to his wife and one each to the two boys. For a few minutes the room was filled with the sound of tearing paper and then of surprised voices.

"That was not necessary, Senhor," Alcino said. It seemed to me that there was a slight reproach in his voice.

"In my country," I said, "when one is first invited to a home, it is customary to take some small gifts."

"Then we thank you," he said, his smile returning.

His wife was looking at the shawl and dabbing at her eyes. Suddenly she turned and left the room.

"My wife," Alcino said, "is very emotional. She always solves it by going to the kitchen and fixing food. Let us sit down."

We sat at the table, leaving the two children to play with their toys on the floor. A moment later, Alcino's wife came in bearing food. She had to make several trips. On the last one, she placed a bottle of clear liquid beside Alcino's plate. Then she coaxed the boys away from their toys and got them to the table. She uncovered a huge dish and a mouth-watering smell floated out of it.

"Senhor," Alcino said, "have you ever had *feijoada completa?*"

"No," I admitted.

"My wife is the best cook of *feijoada completa* in all Brazil. You will see."

The food was dished out and a heaping plateful was put in front of me. It looked a little like stew—I could spot black beans and pieces of various kinds of meat—but the smell was like nothing I'd ever experienced. Alcino leaned over and poured into my glass from the bottle. He filled his own glass, gave a small amount to his wife, and about a thimbleful each to his sons.

"We always drink *pinga* with this dish," he said. He lifted his glass. "To your good health, Senhor March."

I assumed it was some local wine. I lifted the glass and took a good swallow.

Then I found myself fighting for my breath. My throat was on fire and tears were streaming from my eyes. But at least I had finally encountered something that was familiar. It tasted exactly like the white mule I'd once had in the mountains of West Virginia.

"*Pinga* is strong, Senhor," Alcino said with a smile. "But one gets used to it."

"What is it?" I asked as soon as I could talk.

"A whiskey. It is made up in the hills. It is not, you understand, an official whiskey."

"I can see why," I said. I was beginning to recover. "We have whiskey like this in my country also, but I wasn't expecting it."

We ate dinner, which lived up to the advance smells, while Alcino talked about his great love—Rio. It was interesting and I contented myself with eating and drinking and listening. Later we had some fruit and small cups of black coffee. Alcino's wife cleared the table and the boys went back to their toys, while we drank coffee and smoked.

It was Alcino who suggested that it was time for us to go. I summoned up my best Portuguese to compliment his wife on her personal beauty, the quality of her food, and the handsomeness of her sons. The two little boys were pushed forward to thank me shyly once more for their toys. Then Alcino and I were finally in the street again. Dozens of children were still outside, stopping their play to watch the intruder in their small world.

"Thank you, Alcino," I said as we drove away. "It was very thoughtful of you to invite me to your home."

"It was my wife," he said. "She would have made life miserable for me if I had not brought you. Now she will do nothing but talk about her new shawl for the next year. It is I who must thank you, Senhor."

We drove straight back to the hotel. I went upstairs and changed into my evening clothes. I put on the shoulder holster, put the gun into it, and slipped on my jacket. It wasn't too bad. An experienced eye would spot it, but the average person wouldn't know I was carrying the gun.

I went back down to the taxi.

"Where to, Senhor?" Alcino asked.

"You know a club called Uma Figa?"

He nodded.

"Let's try it tonight."

We were there in about fifteen minutes.

Alcino pulled to the curb and pointed ahead. "There it is, Senhor."

It was a fairly modern building. In front of it, just beneath the lights, there was a huge fist with the thumb stuck between the index and middle fingers.

"That is the good-luck charm," Alcino said. "You can buy small ones—in wood, bone, or gold—as souvenirs in the Praça Quinze de Novembro."

"I'll settle for this one," I said.

I started to get out, then stopped as a figure came down the street heading for the club. It was Joseph Sforza. "There's one of my men now," I said.

Alcino leaned forward to peer through the windshield. "Is that the one from the Copacabana Hill Hotel?"

"That's the one. Have you seen him before?"

"Yes. About a week ago. I had him as a passenger a couple of times. Then I think he rented a car. At least, I saw him driving a small car with rental plates."

Sforza turned into the club and vanished. I stayed where I was, curious about something. I got the answer a few minutes later. A car drifted down the street and parked under a tree across the street from the club.

"A police car," Alcino said softly.

"I guessed it," I said. "I think the Lieutenant is keeping a constant watch on all three of them. Well, I'll see you later."

I left the cab and went into the club. The first thing that caught my attention was the sound of good jazz. I was so surprised that I stopped until I'd located it. There was a small combo on a stage, and they were playing Dixieland jazz the way it should be played. The club was about two-thirds full. I looked around and spotted Sforza. He was at the bar, nursing a drink and staring at the mirror in back of the bar. There were about fifteen other people at the bar, but it was a big one and there was still plenty of room. I went over and took the stool next to Sforza. He saw me in the mirror, but he didn't turn his head.

"Aren't your friends joining you tonight, Joe?" I asked, meeting his gaze in the mirror.

"They'll be here," he said wearily. "Why don't you go sit somewhere else?"

"I like it here."

"What the hell are you trying to do to me?" he asked.

I waited until the bartender served me and had moved away. "I don't know what you're talking about."

"The hell you don't. Hanging around me like this, and then acting like we're real pals in front of Pete. He don't like it, and I don't like it."

"You can always solve it. I told you how."

He muttered a four-letter word. "How the hell do you always know where we're going to be?"

"A friendly local cop—who's very interested in what you do."

"How the hell does he always know?"

"Haven't you noticed that you always have company wherever you go? Or do you think that guy is following you around to get your autograph?"

"Cops," he said, making it sound like a word he'd said before. "Who is this cop?"

"I don't think you've had the pleasure of meeting him yet. But I imagine you will, when the time is ripe."

"What the hell does he want?"

"The money—all of it."

"What's he going to do about it?"

"The same thing I am," I said cheerfully. "Wait. Something has to snap sooner or later."

"To hell with both of you. And that New York cop, too." For the first time he turned and looked directly at me. "Now, are you going to move or do I have to? I ain't going to sit next to you."

"If that's the way you feel," I said with a smile, "I'll move." I finished my drink and put the glass down. "I'll see you around, Joe."

I walked down to the far end of the bar, which was almost completely empty. I picked a stool and ordered another drink. From where I sat, I could not only watch Sforza but had a clear view of the entrance. I sipped my drink and waited.

After a while Pete Jackson and the girl came in. They stopped just inside the door while Jackson cased the place. I quickly called the bartender over and pointed out Sforza and said I wanted to buy him a drink. The bartender mixed the drink and took it to Sforza, pointing me out as the buyer. I lifted my drink in salute. I knew that Jackson wasn't missing any of it.

Sforza's face twisted with anger. He shoved the drink away from him so violently that half of it spilled on the bar. He looked around as though he knew Jackson must have entered the room. He got up and went to join Jackson and the girl. The bartender shook his head and started to clean up the bar.

I waited until the three of them were seated at a table, then I left the bar and found a public phone. I called the hotel and asked for Fred Bruce. The operator reported that his room didn't answer. I told her to try the bar. That time it worked.

"Hello," he said a couple of minutes later.

"Fred," I said, "this is Milo. What're you doing?"

"Having a couple of drinks with a girl I met on the beach. What's up?"

"Not much. I'm at a nightclub called Uma Figa. Bring your girl and come over."

He hesitated a minute. "Maybe I'd better come by myself. The New York City Police Department does not include night-clubs in its expense accounts."

"Nonsense," I said. "Bring the girl and I'll give you money for the tab. It'll come out of my expense money, and Intercontinental Insurance can afford it."

"All right," he said. "What do you want me to do?"

"Nothing," I said. "Just bring your girl and have a good time."

"Jackson and Sforza there?"

"Yes."

"Maybe it'll be dangerous to bring the girl."

"No danger. I just want you here for a little extra psychological pressure. Now, listen. I'll make a reservation for you in your name, so merely ask for it. I'll be at a table in the back of the club, but don't come anywhere near me or let on that you know me."

"Why? You already introduced me to them this afternoon."

"Not for their benefit," I said patiently. "Lieutenant Alvares may have some men here, too, and I want them to continue to think that I'm all alone."

"All right."

"Shortly after you come in," I continued, "I will get up and go to the men's room. Wait about two or three minutes and follow me. I'll give you enough money for the evening and then come back. You wait a few minutes before going back to your table."

"That's all?" he asked.

"That's all. I have an idea that not too long after you arrive, Jackson and Sforza and the broad will leave. Then you can just relax and enjoy the rest of the evening with your girl."

"What are you going to do? Follow them?"

"No. I'm going to relax and enjoy myself. These things have to be done with a delicate hand. Put on too much pressure and the situation might fall apart. See you soon." I hung up and went out to find the headwaiter. I pressed a wad of cruzeiros on him.

"I would like a table for myself somewhere in the back of the club, not too far from the music."

"Certainly, Senhor," he said. "Right this way."

"First," I said, "I would also like to make a reservation for a friend of mine who will arrive in twenty or thirty minutes."

"Your friend is not joining you?"

"No. He is accompanied by a young lady, and I think he would prefer to be alone with her."

"Ah," he said with understanding.

I pointed to an empty table not far from the one occupied by Jackson. "I think my friend would like that table. His name is Senhor Bruce."

"Certainly, Senhor. I will take care of it." He made a note on a small pad in his hand. "Now, if the Senhor will follow me ..."

He led me to a table that was across the stage from where Fred would be sitting, only about three tables removed from the orchestra. "How is this one, Senhor?"

"Excellent," I said.

He held the chair for me, then motioned with his hand, and a waiter was there. I ordered a drink and settled back in my chair.

A girl appeared on the stage. I should say a woman. She was tall, with long black hair down to her shoulders and the kind of dark beauty and full figure that you usually find only among Latin women. She was breathtaking.

She sang with the combo, first a hot jazz number in Spanish, then a blues in French, and one in English. She had a fine voice and I was enjoying myself so much that I didn't realize Fred Bruce had come in until she'd finished the one in English.

I sighed and got up. I walked back toward the men's room. I hated to leave just then, but it was a good time because there wouldn't be many people in the restrooms.

It was empty when I got there. I counted out enough money to carry Fred through the evening, folded it up into one hand, and then pretended to be drying my hands on a towel while I waited. I didn't have too long to wait. The door opened and

I saw it was Fred coming in. I dropped the towel and headed for the door.

"Excuse me, Senhor," I said as I slipped by him. I put the money in his pocket and went on out.

She was singing another song as I sat at the table again. She continued to sing for perhaps a half hour. She started to leave the stage, but the applause brought her back. As she started a new song, I beckoned the waiter.

"The singer," I said, "she is very good. What is her name?"

"Carmelita da Silva, Senhor."

"I wonder if she would join me for a drink when she is through?"

He shrugged. "She does not do so often, Senhor. Would you like me to ask her?"

"Yes," I said. I gave him some money.

She sang two more songs, then left the stage. I saw the waiter stop her and gesture in my direction. A moment later she was walking straight for my table. I got to my feet and waited for her to approach.

"Thank you for coming," I said as she reached me. "Won't you permit me to buy you a drink? I am called Milo March."

"Thank you," she said in English.

The waiter, who had followed her, held the chair and she sat down.

"I am Carmelita da Silva. You are an American, no?"

"Yes."

She nodded at the waiter and he left. "Do you mind if we speak English?" she asked. She had a charming accent. "I would like to speak it better than I do."

"Not at all," I said. "My Portuguese is not too good. I enjoyed your singing very much. I hope you don't mind that I asked you to join me for a drink?"

She laughed. "Not at all. You might even be an American movie producer."

"For once in my life I'm sorry I'm not," I said.

She shrugged. "Well, you are still an attractive man and I am here."

The waiter came and put a glass of wine in front of her. I motioned for him to bring me another drink and he left.

"I do two shows," she said. "Until the last one is over I do not drink anything but wine. You liked my singing, no?"

"Yes."

"Someday I will be a big star. Bigger even than Carmen Miranda. That is why I wish to speak better in English."

"I'm sure you will be," I said. "When do you do your next show?"

"In one hour. Then I sing no more. After that people are drinking too much to enjoy good singing, and they have two other singers. Not good voices but what you call hot."

The waiter brought my drink. I lifted it and looked at her. "To a lovely woman with a lovely voice," I said.

"Thank you, Senhor," she said.

We drank, and when she put her glass down it was empty.

"Another one?" I suggested.

She shook her head. "I must go and rest before my next show. I am sorry."

"Perhaps you'll join me again after your next show?"

She smiled. "Perhaps."

I stood up as she left. Then I sat down again and glanced across the stage. I was just in time to see Jackson, Sforza, and the girl leaving. Fred Bruce looked at me as if to ask for orders. I winked at him and leaned back in my chair. Pete Jackson glanced at me on his way out. I waved to him in friendly fashion, but he ignored me.

For a while the orchestra switched to dance music, and many of the customers danced, including Fred Bruce and the girl he was with. Then the group switched back to jazz and Carmelita da Silva appeared again. I lost myself in the music and her voice—I'm an old jazz buff from way back.

When she left the stage she came directly to my table. I stood up until she was seated.

"You were great," I told her. "What would you like to drink?"

"I don't know," she said, looking around. "Do you like it here?"

"I do since you appeared. Why?"

"I don't like to drink in clubs such as this. I would rather be in a quiet place where we could just drink and talk."

"Anything you say."

"Where are you staying, Senhor?"

"The Copacabana Palace."

"They have a nice bar. Why don't we go there?"

I motioned for the waiter. He added up the check and I paid him.

"I will get my coat," she said, "and meet you at the door." She was gone.

I walked up to the front door and waited. Fred Bruce kept

glancing at me as though he felt guilty being left there to enjoy himself. In a couple of minutes the singer was back, a light coat around her shoulders. We went outside.

"I have a taxi waiting," I told her, and we turned down to where Alcino was parked. "Back to the hotel," I told him.

"Yes, Senhor," he said.

We were quiet during the ride, her perfume reaching out to embrace me. When we reached the hotel, I helped her out, then leaned into the cab and gave Alcino his four dollars. "Come tomorrow morning between ten and eleven," I told him.

"Yes, Senhor," he said. His voice was merry. "The Senhor does well by himself."

"Bastante," I said. "I'll see you tomorrow."

I escorted Carmelita into the hotel bar and to a table in the corner. On the way I received several envious glances, which makes any man feel good. She said that she would drink whatever I was having, so I ordered two V.O.'s with soda backed. When they came, she mixed hers. She lifted her glass.

"Thank you, Senhor."

"If you insist on speaking English," I told her, "my name is Milo."

"Thank you, Milo," she repeated with a smile. "Now, tell me all about America."

I was amused. "That's a big order. What do you want to know?"

"Everything," she said.

So I started talking, paying more attention to her reactions than to what I was saying. I had been talking several minutes, and our glasses were empty, when she reached out and put her hand on mine.

"Please," she said. She hesitated a minute, then went on. "Would you think me not a nice girl if I asked could we go to your room and have drinks while we talk? It is noisy here."

"Of course not," I said. I beckoned the waiter and paid him. Then I looked at her. "Would you prefer I buy the bottle down here before we go up?"

She knew what I meant and smiled. "No, Milo. Brazilian waiters are very understanding. If you tip him for two, he will see only one."

We went upstairs. I took her coat and hung it up. I phoned room service and asked them to send up a bottle of V.O., two glasses, a bucket of ice, and some soda.

Carmelita had curled up on the bed and turned on the radio. She adjusted it so that the music furnished a soft background. She fluffed the pillows up against the headboard, kicked her shoes off, and curled her feet up under her full skirt.

"When I am not singing," she said, settling herself against the pillows, "I like to drink and talk. But it is so noisy in most places."

I agreed that it was noisy, and then there was a knock on the door. I went over and let the waiter in. He opened the bottle of V.O., then presented the check. I signed it and gave him a good-sized tip. She'd been right. Never by so much as a flicker of an eyelid did he let on that there were two people in the room. I let him out and poured a drink for her, adding soda. I gave it to her and served myself some V.O. on the rocks, then retreated to the chair.

We had been talking perhaps fifteen minutes when the phone rang. I crossed over to it and answered.

"Senhor," said a voice which I recognized as Alcino's, "I am sorry to disturb you, but I thought you would want to know."

"What?"

"The man you pointed out to me in front of Uma Figa. Someone has just killed him."

EIGHT

For a minute I was stunned. It had occurred to me that Sforza might be slated to follow the other members of the gang, but I hadn't expected it to happen so suddenly or right under the noses of the police.

"How did you find out about it?" I asked Alcino.

"After I left you, I drove by to see a friend of mine. We had a couple of drinks of *pinga* and I started home. I was driving along a quiet street when somewhere ahead of me I heard what sounded like a shot. Then there was a crash. When I reached the spot, there was a car which had run into a lamp-post. There was a crowd around it, but I got in close enough to see the man who was in the car. He was the one you pointed out to me. There was a hole in his head. I slipped away to a telephone just as the police arrived."

"Thanks, Alcino," I said. "Perhaps you'd better make it earlier tomorrow."

"Nine o'clock, Senhor?"

"That should be all right. I have an idea that I will be hearing from our friend after this."

"The Lieutenant?"

"Yes."

"I will be there, Senhor." He hung up.

I replaced the phone and went back to the chair. I thought

about what Alcino had told me.

"Something has happened, Milo?" Carmelita asked softly.

"Something has," I said.

"Would you like me to leave?"

"Oh, no," I said. I had made a decision. I knew that I had a small opportunity that I would never have again. "But would you mind staying here while I go out for about fifteen minutes, no more than twenty?"

"To another woman?" she asked with a smile.

"No woman. This is business."

"I will stay," she said. "I will drink the good whiskey and think of what we will talk about."

"You're a sweetheart," I told her.

I went to the closet and took off my white dinner jacket, standing so she couldn't see the gun. Then I put on the dark jacket of one of my suits. "I'll be back quickly," I said. I went out, locking the door.

I went downstairs and left the hotel by the back entrance. I walked the three blocks to the Copacabana Hill Hotel and went straight to the elevators. No one paid any attention to me.

"Four," I told the operator as the elevator started up.

He let me out on the fifth floor and I walked down to the fourth. I soon found 489. I knocked on the door just to play safe. There was no sound from inside. The corridor was empty.

I pulled a key ring from my pocket. On it there were a number of picks with which it is possible to pick most ordinary locks. It took me two minutes to find the right one and open the door. I used a handkerchief when I turned the knob so there would be no prints. I stepped inside, closing the door and moving quickly to one side of the door at the same time. I waited a minute, but there was no sound in the room. Finally, I turned on the overhead light.

I glanced at my watch and tried to estimate how much time I had. I was assuming that Jackson had killed Sforza. If so, would he dare come directly from the killing to Sforza's room? Probably not. And he might feel sure that he could eventually get whatever share of the money Sforza had stashed. So that left the police. Alcino had said he went to the phone just as the police arrived. They would examine the car and the body and then call in. I was willing to bet that Lieutenant Alvares had left standing orders to notify him of anything that concerned Jackson and Sforza. Anyway, his man was following Sforza—had Joe given his tail the slip? Once Alvares got the news, he'd move quickly, and Sforza's room would be the first place he'd head for. A little more than five minutes had passed since Alcino had called me. At the outside I had twenty minutes, maybe not quite that much.

I went to work. I started in the bathroom. I checked the tank on the toilet, the shower curtains, underneath the sink, then looked in the medicine cabinet. There was nothing there that would hold money. I moved into the other room.

I checked everything on and under the bed. I went over the curtains and looked under the carpeting. I even went over the balcony. I moved on to the drawers in the dresser, pulling it out to look at the back. Every place I searched, I made sure that I left no prints.

There was nothing left but the clothes closet. I opened the door and went through the clothes there. Nothing. The shelf was empty. The only thing on the floor were two pairs of shoes and a new pigskin bag. I opened the bag. It was empty. I closed it and moved it to one side. Suddenly, I stopped. It seemed to me that the bag was heavier than it should be. I glanced at my watch. I'd been in the room for twelve minutes. Time was running out.

I said to hell with it and picked up the bag. I went to the door and used my handkerchief to open it. I looked out. The corridor was empty. I turned off the light and pulled the door shut. I went down along the elevator bank until I came to the one that was marked for bathers only. I knew that one was probably self-operated. I pressed the button and was relieved to see that the car was coming up.

The door opened and I stepped in and pushed the button. It made only one stop, which was in the basement. I put the bag on the floor where it couldn't be seen easily from outside when the door opened. When I got out of the elevator in the basement, there was no one in sight. I picked up the bag and stepped out.

There was an underground tunnel running from the basement under the street and coming out on the beach. I ducked into it as fast as I could. A minute later I was out on the beach getting my shoes full of sand as I trudged in the direction of my hotel. There were a few couples on the beach, but fortunately the light was dim and everyone seemed too preoccupied to pay any attention to me.

Three blocks on the sand seems much longer than three

blocks on concrete, but I finally made it. I crossed through to the hotel and entered at the rear. I stamped my feet to get rid of the outward signs of sand and took an elevator up to my floor. I let myself into the room.

"Hi," I said, and went straight to the closet. I threw the bag on the floor next to my own.

"I didn't know," she said from back of me in Portuguese, "that you were on such a long trip that you needed luggage."

"Oh, that," I said. I was busy slipping out of my jacket and getting the shoulder holster off without her seeing it. "I just suddenly remembered that I'd left a bag in the checkroom downstairs. I thought I might as well bring it up."

"Of course," she said, going back to English. "I understand how you felt."

I had just finished putting the gun and holster out of sight when I realized that her dress was hanging in the closet right next to my suit. I turned to look at her.

She was in bed with the covers pulled up to her chin. She had a drink in one hand and her hair spilled over the pillow like a wind-blown cloud. She smiled at me.

"I made myself comfortable," she said. "Do you mind, Milo?"

"How could I mind?" I asked. I closed the closet door and went into the bathroom. I took each shoe off carefully and emptied the sand into the toilet. Then I brushed my socks over the bowl and flushed it. I put the shoes back on and went into the room.

"I think I need a drink," I said. I poured myself a large one and retreated to the chair. "Did anything happen while I was gone?"

"I had a couple of drinks," she said, "and I made myself comfortable."

"No phone calls?"

"No. Did you expect one?"

"I do now," I said. "Any minute."

I wasn't off by very much. It was less than fifteen minutes before the phone rang. I went over and picked it up.

"Senhor March?" a man's voice asked. I thought I recognized it.

"Yes. Who is this?"

"Lieutenant Alvares. I trust I did not disturb you?"

"Of course not. What would make you think that?"

"I just spoke to the clerk. He seemed to think that you might be entertaining and suggested that I not call you. Is there someone with you, Senhor March?"

"Of course not."

"You are beginning to sound like a Carioca," he said scornfully. "Everyone in Rio is so polite when it comes to the ladies. Well, it doesn't matter. If it is not inconvenient, I would like you to come in to see me in the morning."

"All right. What time?"

"Nine-fifteen or nine-thirty. Good night, Senhor."

"Good night."

I put the phone back and returned to the chair. I took a long drink and relaxed.

"A friend?" she asked.

"Not exactly," I said with a smile. "More like a friendly enemy."

I finished my drink and made myself another one. She was

still working on the one she had, a smile on her face as she watched me.

"If you are not an American movie producer," she said, "perhaps you are an American gangster."

"Not that either."

She sighed. "I had such a romantic notion while you were gone. I imagined that you had spent all your money on me and had gone out to rob someone so as to have more money to spend on me."

"I'm not quite broke yet," I said. I smiled at her. "It must be the music." I nodded toward the radio from which soft, lulling music drifted.

"Perhaps," she said. "If I'm asked, do you want me to say that you were with me all the time tonight?"

"You won't be asked."

"Why did you tell the caller that there was no one with you?"

"I wouldn't involve you," I said.

"That is foolish, if you need to prove where you were."

"I don't think I need to," I said, "but thanks, Carmelita."

She was looking at me, her eyes half-veiled and a little smile on her lips. Suddenly she threw the covers off. She had removed all her clothes.

"Do you think I am beautiful, Milo?" she asked.

I admitted I did.

She swung her feet to the floor and stood up. Then she walked past me, conscious in every movement of her woman-hood, and I heard the bathroom door close. I finished my drink and poured another one. The ice was almost gone.

She came back into the room and got into bed. She pulled the covers up slowly.

"It is nice that you think I am beautiful," she said. "Do you want to know what else I thought about while you were gone?"

"Yes."

"I thought that sometimes I talk too much when there are other things in life." She reached up lazily and put out the light. A small streak of moonlight came through the window, laying a silver lance across the shape of her body beneath the covers.

I finished my drink, undressed, and went to bed.

It was a few minutes before eight when I awakened in the morning. It was several seconds before I remembered that I was not alone. I looked at her. She was still asleep, her face beautiful in repose. I slipped out of bed and went to take a shower. When I returned, she was awake, a smile in her eyes as she looked at me. I unlocked the door and got back into bed.

"What would you like for breakfast?" I asked.

"The same that you have," she said.

I called room service and ordered papaya, scrambled eggs, toast, and coffee for two. She put one arm out from beneath the covers and I held her hand.

It was the same as it had been the night before. The waiter knocked and then entered, wheeling the table ahead of him. He placed it beside the bed and presented the check, all without showing any awareness that I was not alone in bed. I signed the check, adding a generous tip.

"Thank you, Senhor," he said, and marched out.

As soon as I'd finished breakfast, I got dressed. I carried my tie and coat, with the holster beneath the coat, into the bathroom. I put on the holster, tied my tie, and slipped into the coat. Then I went back to the room.

"I have to go out on business," I said. "Stay as long as you want to. I'm not sure what time I'll get back."

"I understand," she said. "Perhaps I will be here when you return, perhaps not. But if I'm not, you will know where to find me."

"I know," I said. I leaned over the bed and kissed her. Her arms went around my neck and the warm, scented sleep-smell engulfed me and made me reluctant to leave. But I did—with her smiling after me from the bed.

Alcino was already waiting in front of the hotel. I got into the taxi.

"Lieutenant Alvares," I said.

He made the U-turn and drove off.

"Thank you for the call last night," I said.

"Did it help, Senhor?"

"I don't really know yet, but I'm glad you made the call."

"The Lieutenant wants to see you?"

"Yes. He phoned me last night, although I think he did that partly to find out where I was."

"He is tricky, Senhor. You must watch him."

"I will," I said.

Alcino parked near the building. He made the sign of the *figa* with his fist as I left. I went inside police headquarters and stopped by the officer at the desk. He recognized me and motioned me to go on up. I mounted the steps and knocked at the door, which was becoming more and more familiar.

"*Entra,*" he called from the other side.

I opened the door and went in. He was sitting in his usual position.

"Ah, Senhor March," he said. "Come in and be seated."

I took the chair next to his desk and lit a cigarette. "Is there something up?"

"Not much," he said casually. "I see you received your permit for the gun without trouble."

"Yes, thank you."

"May I see it?" he asked, holding out his hand.

I took the gun from the holster and handed it to him. "It's loaded," I said, "but there isn't a bullet under the hammer."

"I am glad to see that you are careful with guns," he said gravely. He looked the gun over carefully and I noticed that he sniffed at the barrel. "Where did you buy the gun, Senhor March?"

"From a man."

His eyebrows went up. "Just a man? No name?"

"I think he said his name was Manuel Gaspar."

"And you don't know where he lives?"

"No."

He shook his head. "You are blessed with fortune, Senhor March. Usually such guns have been stolen, but I see we have no record of it. Of course, it is a gun that was made in the United States." He looked at me without raising his head. "Are you sure you didn't bring this gun with you?"

"And break your national laws?" I exclaimed. "How long

would I last in my business if I went around breaking laws?"

"True, true," he said. He sighed heavily. "I dislike to inconvenience you, Senhor, but I must ask you to leave your gun with me for one or two hours."

"Why?"

"A man was killed last night. He was shot through the head with an American-made gun, .38 caliber. He was a countryman of yours."

"Who?" I asked.

"Joseph Sforza." He was watching me closely.

"No!" I said. I wasn't any Spencer Tracy, but I thought I was doing a pretty good acting job. "But I saw him last night—in a nightclub."

"I know," he said. "Uma Figa. You talked to him for a while at the bar. Then you moved to the other end of the bar. Later, you bought him a drink, which he angrily refused."

"And he left at least an hour before I did."

"I also know that, Senhor."

"You had one of your men watching Sforza. How come he didn't get the killer?"

"I regret to say that Senhor Sforza managed to lose my man shortly before he was killed."

"It seems to be a habit of your men," I observed. "At what time was Sforza killed?"

"A few minutes past eleven."

"Then you can hardly think I did it. I was in the bar of my hotel at eleven o'clock and stayed there until about twenty-five after, when I went up to my room—where you phoned me not too much later."

"I know," he said. He was using a pencil to drum on the desk. "I spoke to the bartender who was on duty, to the desk clerk, and the waiter who took a bottle of whiskey to your room. They agree with you. Still, that does not rule you out."

"Why?"

"Being a successful policeman, Senhor—and you will notice that I use the word *successful*, not the word *good*—is an art, not a science. The things that I feel are more often right than the things I think. I feel, Senhor March, that you are a very clever man. And I feel very strongly that you had something to do with the death of Senhor Sforza. So I will keep your gun long enough to compare it with the bullet which killed your countryman."

"What about Sforza's friend, Peter Jackson?"

"I also have feelings about him. I had a long talk last night with Senhor Jackson and the lady who claims to be his wife, then another long talk with them this morning. Unfortunately, he also has what you call an alibi."

"You mean the girl says he was with her?"

"She says so, but if that were all, it would be nothing. There is other evidence."

"How good?"

"When the two men and the girl left Uma Figa, they went directly to the Jogo do Bicho. Two of my men followed them there. Senhor Sforza stayed until about fifteen minutes before eleven, then he left. One of my men followed him and was lost. Senhor Jackson and the girl stayed in the club until well after twelve. One of my men was in front of the club all the time, where he could see both the club doors and Senhor

Jackson's car. The owner of the club and the waiter for that table also bear out the story. I myself first talked to Senhor Jackson at the club shortly after midnight."

"Sounds like a pretty good alibi," I admitted.

"There is something else of interest," he said. "You see, Senhor March, I am being completely honest with you, even though I think you are somehow involved."

He was like hell; he was trying to set the biggest bear trap he could find. "I appreciate that fact," I said gravely.

"I had left word that I was to be notified day or night about anything concerning those three, so I was called at home as soon as the body of Senhor Sforza was identified. I went directly to his hotel room to search it for clues. I arrived there perhaps no more than twenty-five or thirty minutes after Senhor Sforza was shot. I found two strange things. There were no fingerprints on the doorknob, inside or out— no prints of Senhor Sforza, the cleaning woman, a waiter, anybody. Inside the room, nothing seemed disturbed. The Senhor Sforza had considerable clothing, in the dresser or hanging neatly in the closet, but he had no luggage of any sort. Do you not find that interesting?"

"Yes," I said. "I can think of possible explanations, although I am sure you must already have thought of them."

"What?"

"First, the absence of prints. It is possible that Sforza had a record and tried to be careful not to leave any of his prints around. Or it's possible that sometime during the day a thief broke into his hotel room hoping to find something of value—a careful thief."

"And the absence of luggage?"

"Perhaps that is what the thief took."

He shook his head. "It is too easy an answer. In all my life I have never found easy answers."

"I don't know about Rio," I said, "but in New York City there are many places where there are public lockers. One can put in a coin which permits the locker to open. Something even as large as a suitcase can be stored there as long as another coin is put in every twenty-four hours. If Sforza had something of value in his suitcase, he might do something like that."

"There are two places in Rio with public lockers such as you mention," Alvares said thoughtfully. "But where would the key be? We found no such key on the body or in the room."

"There could be several answers to that also. He might have put it in the hotel safe. He might have found someplace to tape it, either in his room or on the car he had rented. Or he might have mailed it to himself in care of General Delivery, marked 'hold' until called for."

"As I said, you are a clever man, Senhor March. Do you know what problem occupied me most of the night?"

"I can't imagine."

"You. First, how could you manage to kill Senhor Sforza, yet have many people swear you were in the hotel at the time he was killed? Then, if you did not kill Senhor Sforza, how could you learn about it quickly enough to get into his hotel room and out before I reached it? I did not find any answers."

"That's because I was more pleasantly occupied," I said with a smile.

"Oh, yes," he said. "Senhor March, I am not as polite as my countrymen. I know who you were with last night, and I may yet question her."

"I cannot tell you what to do," I said. "But you are looking in the wrong direction, Lieutenant."

"Perhaps. We will see. I will talk to you again soon, Senhor March."

"When can I get my gun back?"

"In about two hours—if it does not match the bullet. Thank you for coming in, Senhor."

"Não há de que," I said. I got up and left.

There was a worried look on Alcino's face until he spotted me. Then he broke into a grin and opened the back door.

"All is well, Senhor?" he asked.

"More or less, but my wings have been clipped for at least a couple of hours." I opened my coat to show him the empty holster. "The Lieutenant wants to make sure the bullet didn't come from my gun."

"But he didn't hold you. Where to, Senhor?"

"Let's go back to the hotel."

He nodded and put the car in gear. I twisted on the seat and watched through the rear window. A car immediately pulled out behind us. Then, a moment later, another one pulled out from a side street and fell in behind the first one.

"We are being honored," I told Alcino. "I think the Lieutenant has two of his policemen following us, so that if we lose one, there'll be another on the job."

"Shall we lose both of them?" he asked.

"I don't think so," I said. "It would only make the Lieutenant more eager, so we'll act like innocent citizens."

He nodded. "Does that pig really think that you shot the dead man?"

"I don't know, but I doubt it. I don't think he's too much concerned with the murder. He's more interested in a missing bag from the dead man's room. He thinks there's something of value in it."

"Ah," Alcino said. "Is there, Senhor?"

"I don't know," I admitted. "There is something of value somewhere, and the Lieutenant wants to find it before I do, or at least to be there when I find it."

We reached the hotel and Alcino parked. Looking back, I saw the other two cars parking farther back. "I don't know how long I'll be," I said, "but wait. If nothing else, we'll go back for my gun in a couple of hours."

He nodded.

I went into the hotel and straight up to my room. I was hoping that Carmelita was gone, because I had a lot to do. She was, but her scent was everywhere in the room, as though she'd left part of herself behind so that I wouldn't forget her.

I made sure that the door was locked. I took off my jacket and hung it up. There was still some whiskey in the bottle, so I poured myself a straight drink. I got the pigskin bag from the closet. It seemed to me that it was still a little heavy, although I couldn't be sure. I sat down on the floor and opened the bag. Then I started going over it inch by inch, occasionally prying at a seam with one of the steel picks on my key ring.

Once the phone rang. I answered. It was Fred Bruce. He

was still in his room. I told him to stay there until he heard from me, and hung up.

I went back to work on the bag. I was positive there had to be some sort of answer in it. Jackson and Sforza had gone through two fairly complete searches without anything being found, yet they had to have the money with them.

It took me an hour, but I finally found it. There was a false bottom in the bag, so cleverly made that there was no way to spot it, either in the shape of the bag or in its construction. There were several brass rivets around both the top and the bottom. I had already fooled with them, but on my second time around, it suddenly occurred to me to try something else. And that worked. The rivets on the bottom were all threaded, but it was a reverse thread, and they had to be turned to the right to loosen them.

A moment later, I lifted the false bottom out. In one corner there was a small, flat automatic. The rest of the secret compartment was filled with American money, ranging from fives to one thousand dollar bills.

NINE

There was no time to count it. Most of the bills were still packaged, and it looked to me as if there were two or three hundred thousand dollars in the bag. It could be counted later. Now there was a more urgent problem. So I sat on the floor in front of all that money, sipping my drink and trying to think of an answer.

Finally, I pushed the bag back into the closet. I went downstairs to the cluster of shops. I bought a very attractive briefcase with a good lock. I stopped in another store and bought a large gift box and some fancy wrapping paper. In a third store I bought a large knife. It was meant as a souvenir, but the blade was sharp. And I picked up some sealing wax. Then I went back to my room.

I packed the money and the gun in the briefcase. I locked it, then put sealing wax over the lock. After that, I sat on the floor again and used the knife to cut the pigskin bag carefully into strips of leather. These I packed into the gift box, and then I wrapped it in the fancy paper and tied a ribbon around it. I was ready.

I picked up the phone and called Fred Bruce.

"Milo," I said when he answered. "I'm coming right down. What's your room number?"

He told me and I hung up. I picked up the package and the

briefcase and left the room. The floor maid was in the hall-way.

"You can clean my room now," I told her.

"*Obrigado,* Senhor," she said.

Fred Bruce was on the floor below me. I took the stairs instead of the elevator. A moment later I was knocking on his door. He opened it almost immediately, and I stepped inside.

"What's this?" he asked.

"I'll tell you later. Right now I want you to do something—at once."

"Okay. What?"

"Get your tie and coat on. I'll tell you while you're doing that."

He obeyed without a word. "I have a taxi waiting downstairs," I said. "I'm going to leave this package and briefcase with you and go down to dismiss him. I want you to come down right after me, with both of these, and take the first taxi on the line. I want my driver to get a look at you, and you can make a note of his taxi. Have your driver take you to the corner of Avenida Marechal Floriano and Uruguaiana. Make sure you're not followed. I don't think you will be, but the connection between us may show up at any time. If you are followed, don't go through with the rest of this. You got the place to go to?"

"Yeah," he said.

"Dismiss your taxi when you get there. My driver should be there at about the same time. If he isn't, wait for him. Get into his cab and he'll drive off with you. Then he'll drop you where you can get a cab back here. Leave the package and briefcase with him."

"Got it," he said. "I gather there's a rush on this?"

"You're damn right there is," I said. I left his room and again took to the stairs. I came out in the lobby and went outside. There were four taxis lined up waiting for fares from the hotel. Alcino was back of them in the regular parking zone. One of the police cars was just two cars behind him. As I approached his taxi, I took some money from my pocket. I leaned in at the window.

"I'm giving you your four dollars now," I said, "so it'll look as if I'm paying you off. In a minute a man will come out of the hotel carrying a briefcase and a gift package and take the first taxi in line. His name is Senhor Bruce. You leave as if I've dismissed you. Make sure you're not followed. Go to Avenida Marechal Floriano and Uruguaiana. If he isn't followed, Senhor Bruce will be standing there. Pick him up and drive him a few blocks, again making sure that you're not followed. When you're certain, drop him where he can get another taxi."

"Is that the man?" he asked.

I took a quick glance and saw it was Fred. He was waiting as the first taxi pulled up in response to the doorman's wave.

"That's him. When he gets out of your taxi, he will leave the package and the briefcase behind. Get rid of the package, preferably someplace where it won't be found soon. Then I want you to take the briefcase home and keep it for me. But make sure that nobody's following you, or it could be dangerous. Come back here when you're through."

"All right, Senhor," he said with a broad smile.

I went back toward the hotel. I heard Alcino pulling out,

but I didn't look around. At the entrance, I stopped and exchanged a few words with the doorman about the weather. At the same time, I looked down the street. Both police cars were still parked.

I walked inside and entered the bar, picking a stool where I could see out into the lobby. I ordered a martini and took a deep breath; for the first time that day, I began to relax. I sipped the martini. A moment later, I saw the driver of the first police car scurry through the lobby. He was probably going to make a phone call.

I ordered another martini and suddenly realized that I was hungry. I told the bartender to send the drink to a table for me, and I went in and ordered lunch.

I was eating it when Fred Bruce looked in. He came over and sat down.

"Everything go all right?" I asked.

"Just as it was planned," he said. "What's it all about?"

"I'm not going to give you any details right now. The less you know the better. But those were two things that Lieutenant Alvares wants very badly. They've been in my room all night, and I wasn't sure the good Lieutenant wasn't going to drop in any minute."

"What happened to your gun?" he asked.

"The Lieutenant has it. He wants to see if I killed a man last night."

"Did you?"

I laughed. "No. But a man was killed."

"Who?"

"Joseph Sforza."

He whistled softly. "Who did it? Jackson?"

"That would be my guess. I think Alvares would like to pin it on him, too, but according to Alvares, he has a hell of a good alibi. Incidentally, I hope you do, too."

He was startled. "What do you mean by that crack?"

"It won't be long before Alvares discovers that you and I know each other. He's been very busy since last night, or he would already have found out that you have called my room and that I have called your room. Alvares is a crook, but he's no fool. When he does discover that, he's going to start wondering where you were at eleven o'clock last night."

"I was still at that nightclub. We didn't leave there until one o'clock this morning."

"Fine. Did you have a good time?"

"Great," he said with enthusiasm. Then he frowned. "But I didn't come down here for a vacation. When are we going to do some work?"

"We already have," I told him.

"I haven't."

"Sure you have. Last night, for example. Then you have just finished a very important piece of work."

"What was in that package and briefcase?"

I shook my head. "I'll tell you sometime but not now."

"How the hell do you expect me to feel as if I'm doing anything when all I've done is sit in a nightclub and act as an errand boy? And I don't even know what I'm delivering. Also, I don't like this business of not cooperating with the local police."

"How long have you been a detective?"

"Three years. Before that I was on a beat."

"Why do you think Johnny Rockland told you to do as I said?"

"I don't know."

"You, my fine detective friend, will eventually have to learn two things. One is that a man isn't to be trusted just because he wears a badge. The other is that patience is one of the best qualities a detective can have. Now, why don't you run along to the beach and have a swim? Maybe your girlfriend is there."

"What are you going to do?"

"As little as possible," I said cheerfully. "I may even get a little drunk. If there's any work to be done, I'm going to let it come to me."

He looked even more puzzled. "What kind of a game are you playing?"

"A winning one, I hope," I said. "Now, run along." He went out, shaking his head.

I finished my lunch and had coffee. On my way out, I stopped at the desk. There was a slip that said New York had been trying to call me. There was an operator's number and a number in New York City. The latter was that of Intercontinental. I called the clerk over and told him to tell all the operators that I would not accept any calls from New York.

I went up to my room. The maid had done a good job. There was no sign of leather on the floor where I had cut up the bag. I checked the whiskey. It was pretty low, so I called room service and told them to send me another bottle of V.O. and some ice.

It soon came. The waiter also brought two glasses, and for a brief second looked surprised when he saw I was alone. I signed the check and tipped him. I took off my coat and shoes, turned on the radio, made myself a drink, and stretched out on the bed.

I had a feeling of excitement that I knew well. I always got it when I thought a case was coming to a head. The death of Sforza had stirred things up somewhat, but the disappearance of Sforza's bag should do even more. It would give Jackson another push, and it had certainly put a burr in Alvares's pants. I grinned to myself.

One thing bothered me. I was sure that Jackson had killed Sforza, yet there was the fact that he had an alibi. I knew that Alvares must have checked it thoroughly. But there had to be a flaw in it somewhere.

The phone rang. I picked it up and said hello.

It was Alcino. "Senhor, I am back," he said. "It went well."

"Good."

"The Lieutenant is at the hotel," he went on. "He was talking to the clerk as I came to the phone."

"Fine," I said. "I want you to do something else for me, Alcino."

"What, Senhor?"

"I want you to find out everything you can about the man who owns that nightclub we went to the other night. The one who won all that money and started the club with it. Anything and everything you can learn."

"I'll do it at once, Senhor."

"Come back here when you've finished." I replaced the phone.

I lit a cigarette and leaned back, sipping my drink. For the moment there was nothing to do but wait.

It wasn't too long a wait. I was only on my second drink when there was a knock on my door.

"Come in," I called. I had left it unlocked.

The door opened and Lieutenant Alvares stepped in. "I wasn't sure I'd find you in, Senhor March," he said.

"Why not?" I asked. "I don't believe in working hard unless I have to. Take a chair and have a drink." He sat down and looked at the bottle.

"Perhaps one," he said.

I waved to the bottle. "Help yourself, Lieutenant."

He took the extra glass, dropped in some ice, and poured it half full of whiskey. He lifted the glass and looked at the color. "You were expecting company, Senhor?"

"No. I just like to be prepared if someone drops in."

He smiled and took a drink. "It is unusual to find a man in his room drinking alone. Celebrating, perhaps?"

I shook my head. "Nothing to celebrate. Since you were so interested in me and my gun this morning, I thought I ought to stay close to the hotel until you had satisfied yourself. I didn't feel like swimming. I did feel like relaxing and drinking."

"That reminds me," he said. He brought my gun from his pocket and held it out. "The bullet didn't match your gun. Since I was coming over this way, I thought I might bring it to you and save you a trip."

"That was kind of you," I said. I examined it to make sure it was still loaded, then slipped it into the holster.

"It is a fine gun."

"Yes. I think I got a good buy on it."

He finished his drink and put the glass down. "I have recently discovered an interesting thing, Senhor. The records downstairs show that you received a phone call from outside the hotel last night five or ten minutes after Senhor Sforza was shot."

"Oh, did I? I don't suppose that I connected the two things because I didn't know about Sforza until you told me this morning."

"Of course. Who was it that called you, Senhor?"

"You know, I'm not sure," I said with a smile. "Some acquaintance, I think, who wanted me to join him in a club. I'm afraid that I had already had too much to drink."

"And, of course, you had more charming company here. I regret it, Senhor, but I would like to look around your room."

"I suppose," I said, "that you have all the necessary papers and that sort of thing, or are they necessary in your country?"

"They are not usually necessary, but since you are a citizen of a friendly country, I took the precaution of getting a search warrant. We would not want to cause an international incident."

"I should say not," I agreed.

"You would like to see the document?"

"If I may."

He took a paper and handed it to me. I scanned it quickly. "Go right ahead, Lieutenant. You won't mind if I don't get up?"

"Not at all. I would not like to inconvenience you." He went to work while I watched. As I had guessed, he was thorough—and neat. He put everything back the way he found it. Finally, he returned to the chair, a bleak smile on his face. He motioned toward the bottle. "May I?"

"By all means," I said. I waited while he poured a drink, then I poured one for myself. "Satisfied, Lieutenant?"

"Of one thing," he said. "Your cleverness. I have the feeling that you are constantly one step ahead of me. I do not like this."

"How can I be one step ahead of you when we're not going in the same direction? I wanted to talk all three of them into voluntarily returning to the United States. You only want to find … what they're doing, and make sure they do not break any of your laws."

His smile grew broader at my pause in the middle of the sentence. "You and I understand each other, Senhor March," he murmured. "I checked your suggestions about the missing luggage, and I'm afraid that there is no evidence to support any of them. The best possibility still seems to be that someone removed the luggage from the room. It must have been someone who knew what the luggage contained and knew that Senhor Sforza was either dead or soon would be."

"Well, you know where I was during the time period."

"Yes," he said gloomily.

"By the way, what was in the luggage?" I asked.

He shrugged. "I do not know, but it must have been valuable. Have you received your New York call yet, Senhor March?"

"No. I have told the operators I will not accept it."

"But why?"

"I don't feel like trying to explain why I haven't accomplished my mission yet."

"I see. The records show also that there have been calls between you and a Senhor Bruce on the next floor. Is he by any chance a fellow worker of yours?"

"No. Merely an acquaintance from New York, here on his vacation."

"Is he in business back in New York?"

"No. He is in civil service that is, he has some sort of job with the city."

"A friend of yours," he said musingly. He was watching me closely. "A friend might agree to keep something in his room for a day or two. Perhaps I should look through his room."

"Go ahead," I said. "I think you'll find him down on the beach."

"I think I may," he said. "Thank you, Senhor."

"It was nothing," I said.

"I will see you again, Senhor," he said as he went out. I got up and locked the door. It was still no more than the middle of the afternoon. I turned the radio down and went to sleep.

I was awakened by the phone. As I fumbled for the receiver, I looked at my watch. It was a few minutes past four. I lifted the receiver and said hello.

"I am back, Senhor," Alcino said.

"Stay where you are," I said. "I'll be right down." I put on my shoes and jacket and tightened my tie. I took a quick look from the balcony. The two police cars were still in front. I went downstairs. Alcino was standing by the house phones. I brushed past him. "Wait," I said.

I went to the back entrance and looked out. There was a car parked there with a man sitting in it. I decided he was probably a policeman, too.

Back by the house phones, I stopped in front of Alcino. "I think there is also a policeman at the back, and I want to get out of here without being followed. What is the next hotel along the beach in that direction?" I nodded in the direction away from the Copacabana Hill.

"There is a small hotel called the Imperial. It is not far, perhaps two blocks."

"Do they have a bar?"

"A small one."

"I can think of only one way out of here without being seen—along the beach. Are there many taxis out front?"

"There were none when I came in."

"Good. Go out and take the first fare the doorman has for you. It'll probably be a short trip this time of day. And it'll throw the watching policeman off. I'll get to the Imperial some way and wait for you in the bar. As soon as you can get there, tell the doorman to notify me."

"All right, Senhor." He turned and went out.

I didn't think anyone was watching inside the hotel, but I went back upstairs just to play safe. While I was there, I went in and turned on my light beside the bed, so that if I didn't get back before dark, they would think I was still in my room. I went out and took the bathers' elevator down to the basement, then walked to the beach. I passed several bathers who looked at me curiously, but that was all.

The beach was crowded, and I was the only person in street

clothes. I walked along at the back of the beach, keeping a watch for Fred Bruce. He was going to be my excuse for being there if anyone was watching. Finally, I saw him lying under a huge umbrella with the same girl I'd seen him with the night before. He looked up and I motioned with my head for him to join me. He said something to the girl and came over.

"Something wrong?" he asked.

"No. Did Lieutenant Alvares come out to the beach to see you?"

"There hasn't been anyone. Why?"

"He came to see me with a search warrant. He'd discovered that there'd been phone calls between our rooms. After he'd searched my room, he wanted to know about you. I said you were a friend of mine and we'd met down here by accident. I told him you had some sort of civil service job in New York City. He left, threatening to search your room. If he's around, just be sure that you don't tell him anything."

"Okay. Look, I'm sorry about today."

"That's all right, Fred."

"I called Lieutenant Rockland after I left you."

"From the hotel?" I asked.

"No. I have more brains than that. I went to a public phone in another hotel and called him collect."

"What happened?"

"He chewed me out," he said ruefully. "He told me not to ask you too many questions, because I might get some answers we wouldn't know what to do with."

I smiled. "That sounds like Johnny. Okay, I'll see you later."

"Is that all you came down here for?" he asked in surprise.

"No. I'm dodging cops. There are three cops tailing me, and I want to get away from them."

"Where are you going?"

"I don't know at the moment," I said honestly. "But wherever it is, I don't want a squad of cops tailing me."

He laughed. "I'll stay around the hotel in case you need me."

"Thanks," I said.

I continued along the beach, getting my shoes full of sand again, becoming too hot beneath the glaring sun. I drew a lot of amused glances, but no cops that I could see. Finally, I saw the Imperial sign across the road, and then the entrance to the hotel from the beach. I took it, and as soon as I was on concrete I stamped off the sand from the outside of my shoes and brushed it from my pants. I was attracting enough attention as it was without trying to empty the shoes, so I put up with sand in them.

I found the bar, a small but pleasant one. There were only three customers there. I sat on a stool and enjoyed a cold martini after my march in the sun.

I had just finished it when the doorman appeared. "Is there a Senhor March here?" he asked.

I left some money on the bar and went out with the doorman. I tipped him and got into the cab.

"They paid no attention to me after they saw I was taking a regular fare," Alcino said as he pulled away. "Where to, Senhor?"

"Turn down a quiet street and park while we talk, and then I'll decide."

He turned at the next corner and parked on a little tree-lined street.

"Did you get any information?" I asked when he had turned the motor off.

He nodded vigorously. "His name is José Eiríco Fonesca. He worked as a waiter and used all of his money to gamble. He never had much luck until the time I told you about. The nightclub has made much money since he opened it. When he first started, he had very grand ideas about making the club larger and putting in a big show that would be finer than anything Rio ever saw. But he has never done it."

"Why?"

"Senhor Fonesca has two weaknesses—gambling and women. His club makes a lot of money, but he gets rid of it as fast as it comes in—even faster."

"What do you mean?"

"He likes to gamble on everything—the animal game, horses, football games, cards. He has had a very bad streak for the last year, and it is said that he has borrowed heavily on the club. In spite of this, he has once more started talking about making the club larger."

"That is interesting," I said.

"That is not all, Senhor," Alcino said. "I told you that his other weakness is women. One of the waiters says that Fonesca's newest interest is the woman with Senhor Jackson."

"*That* is interesting," I said. "Did the waiter say what made him think so?"

"He says that the woman often goes back to Fonesca's office

and that Jackson doesn't seem to care. Do you wish to go see him, Senhor?"

"I don't think so," I said slowly. "That was my idea when I came out, but I think we'll play it differently. Do you know what Jackson and the girl look like?"

"I think so. Last night, they were the couple who arrived also followed by a policeman, no?"

"Yes. You'd know them if you saw them again?"

"Yes, Senhor."

"Night before last," I said, talking more to myself than to him, "they went to Jogo do Bicho. Last night they went to Uma Figa, but left because I was there. Tonight, they should go back to Jogo do Bicho. But they may go somewhere else just to get away from me. ... Alcino?"

"Senhor?"

"Do you know any of the employees at the Copacabana Palace Hotel?"

"My mother's cousin is the doorman. That is why I was able to get a fare so quickly."

"I mean on night duty."

He thought a minute, then his face brightened. "My cousin's nephew. He is a porter, what you call a bellboy. I think that he works at night."

"Would he do something for me? I'll be glad to pay him."

"He'll do it. What do you want?"

"If he could let me know when Jackson and the girl leave the hotel, it might be a big help. But don't go to the hotel. Phone him."

"I can do better than that," Alcino said. "I can catch him

before he goes to work and tell him. You will be in your room?"

"I'll stay there until I hear from him or from you."

"You want me to go somewhere else?"

"Yes. To Jogo do Bicho. Stay outside in your cab. If you see them enter, get to a phone and call me. Even if the boy calls me, I'll wait for your call, at least long enough to give them time to reach the club. Incidentally, what's your cousin's nephew's name?"

"Manuel." He smiled. "Half of the men in Brazil and in Portugal are named Manuel.* You want me to take you back to the hotel, Senhor?"

"No. Take me to a place where I can get another taxi. That way they won't get the idea that you're deeply involved. One more thing. Do you know if there is a back entrance to Uma Figa?"

"There is, but it is not often used."

"All right. If they show up at the other club, you call me, then get over to Uma Figa. At the back door. I'll take another taxi there and let the cops follow me. I'll go through the club and get into your taxi."

"It is good, Senhor," he said. He started the motor and we drove off. He dropped me a half block from where several taxis were parked. I walked down to them and took the first one. It let me out in front of my hotel. I smiled to myself as I went in, knowing how the two cops must be reacting at the sight of me.

---

* Sadly, no longer true. Today, half the men are more likely to be named Gustavo or Bruno.

I stopped to pick up a newspaper and a magazine and then went on up to my room. I checked the ice. It was all melted. I called room service and asked them to send up some ice and a dinner menu.

The waiter came with the bucket of ice. He gave me a menu. "Do you wish to order now, Senhor?"

I looked at my watch. It was a few minutes past five. "I'll order now, but don't bring it for an hour." I ordered a steak, salad, and coffee. I didn't want to eat too much; I had no idea what was going to be ahead of me that night.

When the waiter was gone, I took off my shoes and jacket and assumed my favorite position on the bed. I poured a drink and lit a cigarette.

It was going to be touch and go. I knew that Lieutenant Alvares was getting nervous. Another little push from me and he might decide not to use me as his bird dog any longer. That would make it tough for me, so I had to try to wind it up before Alvares reached that point. It was going to be risky, but I couldn't think of any alternative.

I rested and waited. I had a couple more drinks, but I was taking it easy. A little after six the waiter brought my dinner. I ate slowly and then I had my coffee. I went back to waiting.

It was eight o'clock when the phone rang. I picked it up and answered.

"Senhor March?" a strange voice asked.

"Yes."

"This is Manuel. They just left."

"*Obrigado.* Do you know their room number?"

"Six forty-two."

"Your relative will have something for you tomorrow," I said, and hung up. I didn't know whether the Lieutenant had arranged to have my phone calls tapped or not, but that was a chance I had to take, too.

I went back to waiting. It was twenty minutes before the phone rang again. I picked it up.

"Senhor, it is as you said." It was Alcino. He had already learned to be careful.

"I'll meet you right away. Wait for me." I hung up. Then I moved swiftly. I put on my jacket and shoes and stepped out into the hallway. There was no one in sight. I went to the stairway and climbed two flights. I opened the door a crack and looked out. The hallway was empty. I walked to the door of Jackson's room. Then I stopped suddenly. If there was going to be a trap, this is where it would be. If the Lieutenant believed that I had taken the bag from Sforza's room, as he seemed to, then it would be logical for him to think I would try to get into Jackson's.

I stepped on down to the next room. I knocked softly on the door. There was no response. I took out my picks and soon had the door unlocked. I used my handkerchief and opened the door. I stepped inside and closed it. I waited a minute. There was no sound, and as my eyes adjusted to the darkness, I could see the room was empty. I walked through the room and stepped out on the balcony. The moon was not yet up, so it was dark there, too.

There was no more than a foot between the two balconies. I leaned over the one I was on and listened carefully. There was no sound from Jackson's room. Finally, I climbed from one balcony to the other. Again I stopped to listen. Nothing.

I decided to take a chance. I slipped into the room, moving quickly to one side. I waited once more. But this time I was sure there was no one else in the room. That didn't mean that there still wasn't a trap. I knew what I was looking for. I moved across to the clothes closet. I leaned inside and used my cigarette lighter to look around. There were several pieces of luggage. None was pigskin. But there was an alligator bag that looked exactly like Sforza's pigskin one in every other respect. I had intended to examine the luggage carefully, but now I changed my mind. I picked up the alligator bag and extinguished the lighter. I backed out of the closet and headed for the door. Then I heard the murmur of voices outside.

I turned swiftly and went back to the balcony. It took only seconds to drop the bag onto the other balcony and follow it. I picked it up and entered the room next to Jackson's. I walked over to the door and listened. I could still hear the voices, but couldn't make out any of the words. I put the bag down and, using my handkerchief, opened the door a mere crack. The first voice I heard was that of Lieutenant Alvares.

"... sure that he would be up here by this time," he was saying fretfully. "I don't understand it."

"Why don't we go inside and see if anything's been touched, sir?" another voice asked.

"Because then we'd have to start all over again," the Lieutenant said. He sounded as if he were explaining something to a very backward child. "We examined the lock on Sforza's door and we are certain it was opened by some steel instrument, not a key. So, earlier, while I was inside talking to the Jacksons, Borros put a fine network of tiny threads across the lock outside. You cannot see them, but there is no way to unlock the door without breaking them. They aren't broken; therefore he has not yet entered the room. If we used a pass-key, then we'd break them and the job would have to be done all over again."

"If you can't see them, Lieutenant, how can you tell they haven't been broken?"

"I meant," the Lieutenant said with great restraint, "that you can't see them unless you look closely and know what to look for. He hasn't been here yet. But we know that Senhor March is still in the hotel. We have every exit guarded. I am positive that he will try to enter the room. But even if he does get in and out, it will be impossible for him to move anything out of the hotel. Let's go downstairs and make sure the guards are all in place."

I eased the door shut and waited until after I heard the distant clang of the elevator door. Once more I eased the door open slowly. The hallway was again empty. I went out fast, closing the door behind me, and hurried to the stairs. I went down the two flights and slowly opened the door into the corridor there. It was clear. I went into my own room and locked the door. I dropped the alligator bag on the floor and took the first breath I'd had in many minutes. Then I went over and poured myself a stiff drink and threw it down in one gulp.

The first thing was to find out if I had made the trip for nothing. I opened the bag. It was, of course, empty. But it had the same brass rivets that had been in the pigskin bag. And I soon discovered that they worked the same way. I unscrewed all of them and lifted out the false bottom. The section was completely filled with money, good American currency.

Well, I had the rest of the money, but the Lieutonant had me bottled up.

One thing at a time, I told myself firmly. I took the money out of the bag. Temporarily, I put it on the shelf in my closet and threw a couple of dirty shirts over it. I went back and replaced the false bottom in the suitcase. That left me face to face with the two problems I didn't know how to solve.

One was the bag. I couldn't keep it in my room and I couldn't take it anywhere. Then I had an idea, a risky one, but good if I could get away with it. I shoved the bag in my closet, then went to the door and checked the hallway. No one there. I went out and rang the bell for the self-service elevator reserved for bathers. It came up immediately. I opened the door and then used a pack of matches to keep it from closing. Inside, I reached up and unscrewed the one screw that held the small, square escape hatch in the roof of the elevator.

Leaving the door partly open, I went back to the room and got the bag. I returned to the elevator and got the bag up through the hatch, so that it would rest on the top of the elevator. I hurriedly replaced the hatch and screwed it tight. I picked up the pack of matches and went back to my room. When I reached it, I was soaked with sweat.

The phone was ringing as I came in. Cursing, I raced for it. But when I answered, I managed to sound sleepy.

"Milo," he said. "This is Fred."

I thought of a few choice names to call him, too, but I didn't. "Oh, hello, Fred," I said. I yawned.

"Were you asleep?" he asked.

"I guess maybe I dozed off."

"Everything all right?"

"Everything is fine. I had a few drinks and a nice rest. How's everything with you and your girl?"

"Okay," he said uncertainly.

"Good." I said. "Have fun." I put the receiver down.

I took off my shoes and hung up my coat. I took off the shoulder holster and hung it on the closet door, which was half open. My shirt was wet, so I took it off and tossed it up with the other dirty laundry that covered the money.

I was going to take a shower, but first I went over and sat on the edge of the bed. I poured a drink and started to sip it as I tried to find some answer to the second problem, the money. There was probably close to three-quarters of a million dollars. A lot of it was in big bills, but I still couldn't just put it in my pocket and walk out. How the hell was I going to get that much money out of the hotel when it was swarming with cops? And I didn't see how I could leave it where it was either. Alvares might decide to search my room again.

There was a knock on the door. I sighed and went over and opened it. Lieutenant Alvares was standing there.

TEN

He was the last person I was expecting at the moment. I did think he might drop up later, but I was surprised that he would come while he was waiting for his trap to be sprung.

"May I come in, Senhor March?" he asked.

"By all means," I said. "Forgive me for not asking you first. I'm afraid that I'm thinking a little slowly."

He came into the room and looked around. I saw that his gaze passed over the holster and gun hanging on the door, my suitcase in the closet, and the dirty laundry on the shelf. "I trust I didn't awaken you," he said.

"No," I said. "That was done about two minutes ago by a friend of mine phoning me. A drink, Lieutenant?"

"I would like one, yes." He sat down in the chair.

I gave him a drink on ice and sat down on the bed. I lit a cigarette.

"What did your friend want?"

"He was having fun with his girl, and I guess he thought something was wrong because I wasn't doing the same."

"Sounds like a normal question," Alvares said casually. "Why aren't you?"

"You should know," I said. "She's working. I may go over later and see her. You are working rather late, Lieutenant."

"It's been a long day," he said. "But we don't like to have

murders in our city. I don't think I told you that we discovered the car that was used in the killing—abandoned only a few blocks away. It had been stolen earlier. There were no prints in it. The ignition wires had been torn loose and wired together to make it run, since there were no keys in it. I believe that is a method common in America."

"It was thirty years ago," I said. I looked at him. "So you're looking for a murderer. You seem to be spending much of the day here in the hotel. Do you think your killer is here?"

He smiled. "My only two suspects are staying here. Unfortunately, they both have alibis."

I decided it was time for a change of tactics. "Tell me, Lieutenant, did you come up here for any reason other than a drink? Did you perhaps think I had fled from the balcony by means of knotted bedsheets? Or did you want to search my room again? If that's it, go ahead. Only get it over with. I'm not running an open house."

He finished his drink and put the glass down. "You are a strange man, Senhor March," he said. "You come down here to get three people you claim are murderers. One of them apparently shoots at you. But you spend most of your time in bars, nightclubs, or on the beach. And when it looks as if something is happening that might help you break your case, you spend the afternoon and evening in your room, drinking and sleeping. Yet you are obviously successful in your profession. How is this possible?"

"I make out, Lieutenant," I said.

"I'm sure you do," he replied softly. He stood up. "I have never doubted it. The question which bothers me is—how?

Well, I must go. Unfortunately, I cannot do my job in that manner."

"I'll teach you sometime," I said with a smile.

"You are kind," he said, but he didn't mean it. He gave me a sort of salute as he went out.

I went into the bathroom and showered and shaved. When I came out, I put on the evening clothes—all except the jacket. Then I sat down and stared at the spot where the money was concealed. I had to face one thing. I didn't have a chance of getting the money out of the hotel then. I would have to take my chances on leaving it in the room. There was no point in trying to be elaborate, I decided. But I didn't like where I had it. It would be natural for someone to just grab the dirty shirts and throw them to one side.

I took the money and stacked it neatly on the floor in one corner of the closet.

I put my suitcase up against it, which pretty well concealed it. Then I threw the newspaper on top, and at least it wasn't in sight. Maybe I could get away with it. I put on the holster and gun and then my jacket. I said a small prayer over the closet and left.

The lobby seemed normal until you took a closer look. There were too many men hanging around who didn't look quite comfortable in the clothes they were wearing. I headed for the front entrance. Lieutenant Alvares appeared just before I reached it.

"Ah, Senhor March," he said. "Going out?"

"That was the general idea," I said. "Any objections?"

He spread his hands. "Why should I object, Senhor? We

expect the guests of Rio to enjoy themselves." In the meantime, his gaze was traveling over me inch by inch. I was smiling when his eyes finally met mine. "You find it amusing, Senhor?" he asked coldly.

"Yes," I said. "I suppose if I were guilty of anything, I wouldn't. Obviously, you're looking for more than a killer, but I'll be damned if I know what. All I know so far is that you think some luggage has been stolen. I could hardly carry it under a dinner jacket. You've searched my room and threatened to search that of a friend of mine. I'm sure that you've learned that I have nothing in the hotel safe. But what is it you're looking for?"

"I'm not sure," he said. "I believe you have better knowledge of that than I do." He looked past me toward a man who had just come out of the elevator. The man shook his head and the Lieutenant sighed. "If there was one thing I was certain about, Senhor March, it was that you were a man of action. And now you disappoint me in that. You may go."

"Thank you," I said seriously. I stepped around him and went outside.

The doorman waved up a taxi for me. I got in and told the driver to take me to Uma Figa. As we drove off, I saw that I had my regular escort of two cars.

When we arrived, I paid the driver and went directly into the club. It was pretty well filled, and the orchestra was playing dance music. I knew that Carmelita's first show was over. I went to the back of the club and found the waiter who had served me the night before.

"Is Carmelita da Silva here?" I asked him.

"In her dressing room, Senhor."

"Would you give me a table and tell her that I am here. Then bring us two drinks. Mine is V.O."

He led me to a table, then disappeared in the back. Carmelita and the drinks arrived at the same time.

"I thought you weren't coming," she said.

"I've been busy," I said, "and I still am. I'm going to leave in a minute. I will try to get back by the time your second show is over." I took out my key and put it on the table. "If I'm not, will you go to my hotel room and wait for me?"

She smiled as she took the key. "Did you think I would say no?"

"I was hoping you wouldn't. I don't think I will be in Rio much longer."

Her smile faded. "When will you leave, Milo?"

"I don't know. Maybe tomorrow, maybe the day after. When you get to my room, don't let anyone in. I will knock three times when I arrive."

"All right," she said meekly.

I finished my drink. "I want to leave the club by the back way. Is that near your dressing room?"

"I will show you," she said.

I left money on the table and followed her to the back. She stopped at the end of the corridor. "Here is my dressing room. And there is the way out." She pointed to a door just in front of me. "I will see you later, then?"

"Yes."

"I will wait," she said softly. She squeezed my hand and was gone through the door of the dressing room.

I pushed through the other door and found myself outside. Alcino's taxi was parked only two feet away. I opened the door and got in.

"Senhor," he said, "I was beginning to worry about you."

"I was busy," I said. "Let's go back to Jogo do Bicho. The police are in front."

"All right, Senhor." He started the car, made a sharp turn, and drove up a side street. There was no one behind us as he made another turn.

He parked near the entrance of the club and I went in. I stopped just inside the door and looked around. Pete Jackson and the girl had a table near the bandstand. When the headwaiter came up to me, I pointed out the table I wanted. It was just across the bandstand from Jackson and the girl. He led me to the table, and they spotted me before I reached it.

I sat down and ordered a drink. Jackson and the girl were talking, being careful not to look directly at me. I wanted to talk to the club owner, but there was no hurry. In the meantime, I relaxed and watched them. Jackson was scowling and obviously arguing about something, but he finally gave up and stared sullenly at the band. Then he finished his drink and got up. He left the table without a word to her and walked to the front and out the door. I wondered what was going on.

I didn't have to wonder long. She stood up and walked around the bandstand. She walked as though aware that every man in the place was watching her. She wore a tight-fitting evening gown, and I would have bet she didn't have anything on under it.

Then I was surprised. She was coming directly to my table. I stood up as she reached it.

"Hello," she said.

"Hello, Betty," I said. "Will you join me?"

The waiter was already there, holding the chair for her. She sat down, and I told the waiter to bring us two drinks.

"That's quite a gown you're wearing," I told her. "But I was wondering where you buy your underthings."

She laughed. "I was born in them."

"I'll bet they didn't look the same then. You know, you're liable to start a riot in Latin America dressed like that."

"What about with you?"

"You might even start a small riot with me. Where's your boyfriend?"

"We had an argument and I sent him out to cool off."

"What can I do for you?" I asked her.

"That depends on you," she said.

I smiled. "In what way, honey?"

"I've been watching you," she said. "You're a good-looking guy and you're a smart operator. You've been scaring Pete and Joe to death."

"Somebody certainly succeeded with Joe."

She made a face. "He was a jerk. So is Pete."

"Meaning that I didn't scare you?"

"No. You interested me. You and I could go places together."

"Like New York City?"

She laughed. "I like it here. I had something else in mind."

"A roll in the hay?"

"That could go along with it," she said. "You got Joe's

money, didn't you?"

"Why do you say that?"

"It had to be you. We didn't get a chance to get it and neither did that hungry cop. That leaves you. I don't know how you did it, but you had to be smart to get away with it."

"Suppose I did?" I said. "Where does that leave us?"

"So you've got about a quarter of a million dollars cash. How would you like to parlay it into an even split of everything?"

"You and me?"

She nodded. "And the same in the future. You know the insurance racket, and we could make it big."

"What about Pete Jackson?"

She laughed. "That's easy. We just tip that cop Alvares off to where he can find the gun that killed Joe Sforza. He takes care of the rest of it for us."

"And Pete goes the way of Eddie and George and Tony and Joe?"

"That's the idea. It's always been the idea."

"When would it be my turn to take the same route?" I asked.

"Never, baby. You're smart. And I'm sick of jerks who get scared by their own shadows."

"Let me get something straight," I said slowly. "I've been under the impression that everything that's happened was Jackson's idea. That he wanted the million dollars for just the two of you."

"Are you kidding?" she said scornfully. "All you have to do is look at his record. He was never anything but a small-time crook. He never copped more than three or four thousand in his life. I was the one who figured out the job, planned it, and made them carry it out. I was the one who figured how we'd get away with it and where we'd go. And it took me two years to puff him up to be a big enough man to do what I told him. Then you come along and all the wind goes out of him. Joe, too. He wanted to make a deal with you."

"So do you."

"Not that kind of deal. One that will put both of us in clover."

"I'll admit that the idea of being in clover with you has a certain appeal," I said. "But the other thing needs a little more talking, and this is not the place. Let's both sleep on it and get together in the morning."

"All right," she said. She finished her drink and leaned across the table so that there wasn't any doubt about what was beneath her dress. "We can make it big, Milo—in every way. I'll call you in the morning."

"You do that, honey," I said.

I stood up and watched her leave. Then I sat down again. It was an interesting twist she had just introduced. Up to then I'd been thinking of her as just a dumb blonde. But there was a ring of truth in what she said. None of the men, including Jackson, had ever pulled any big jobs before. And none of their jobs had needed or demonstrated any brains.

Jackson returned and sat at the table with Betty, scowling. She began talking to him and it seemed to work. He relaxed and looked more normal. Finally, they got up and danced.

I beckoned the waiter over. "Is Senhor Fonesca around?" I asked.

"I think he is in his office, Senhor."

"I would like to talk to him. Tell him that I am the American he spoke to about the mountain that fell on the apartment house."

The waiter nodded and went away. He was back five minutes later. "Senhor Fonesca suggests that you step back to his office. You will find it just beyond the restrooms."

"Thank you," I said. I got up and walked toward the rear.

I found the door, clearly marked, just beyond the men's room. I knocked on it gently.

"Entra," he called.

I opened the door and stepped inside. It was a small, cluttered office. Fonesca sat behind a desk piled high with papers.

"Come in, Senhor, come in," he said. "I trust there is nothing wrong?"

"No. I am merely hoping that you can satisfy my curiosity."

"If I can, Senhor."

"I am interested in the matter that brought the police here last night."

A wary look came into his eyes. "The Senhor is also a policeman?"

"No. Just say that I am interested. I understand that the Senhor Jackson was at his table all during the time in which the police were interested?"

"That is true."

"You and the waiter both observed him to be there?"

"Yes, Senhor."

"But I noticed one thing missing from what Lieutenant Alvares said. Perhaps he did not question this so much. But

I did not hear that the young lady was also at the table all the time."

"She did not leave the club," he said. "I am sure of that, Senhor."

"But she was not at the table all the time?"

"She may have gone to the ladies' room. One does not observe such things closely."

"Of course not. But did she go to the ladies' room?"

He was uncomfortable. "I think perhaps she did. I am not sure."

"I have heard," I said, "that you are interested in the young lady."

"I have observed that she is beautiful, that is all," he said. "She is the wife of the Senhor Jackson."

"So I've heard," I said. "I also am told that you are thinking of enlarging your club."

He seemed grateful to have the subject changed. "Oh, yes. That is what I am doing now, going over the estimates. We expect to give out the contracts tomorrow."

"We?"

"A manner of speaking, Senhor. I mean I will give out the contracts tomorrow."

"It must be an expensive operation."

"Oh, yes. It will cost almost sixty million cruzeiros, but then I will have the finest club in Rio."

"I congratulate you," I said. "Good night, Senhor."

"Good night," he said. He was still staring after me as I walked out and closed the door.

I settled my bill with the waiter and left the club. "Back to the hotel," I told Alcino as I climbed into the cab.

We rode several blocks while I pondered my chief worry. "Alcino," I said finally, "I have a problem that I cannot solve."

"What is that, Senhor?"

"There is something in my room which I must get out by the latest tomorrow morning. Tonight it is impossible, because the hotel is full of police, most of them watching me. Even if there are not so many police in the morning, there will certainly be many outside, and they will be most interested if I appear with a package. Do you have any suggestions?"

"How large is the package, Senhor?"

"About this large," I said, showing him the size with my hands as he looked around. "But it doesn't have to be that shape."

"Could it be carried in a bag?"

"Yes, but not just by itself. The shape would be suspicious."

"With clothing around it?"

"Yes. That might do it. What do you have in mind, Alcino?"

"My cousin's nephew. He gets off in the morning. Sometimes he carries his uniform home to be cleaned—in a bag."

"Is that the one who called me tonight?"

"Yes."

"Then you better find out first if he has been questioned. I don't know if the Lieutenant had someone listening to my phone calls or not."

He nodded. The first place we came to where there was a public phone, he stopped and made a call. He came back and started the motor. "He has not been questioned."

"Then it may be safe. What times does he leave in the morning?"

"Eight o'clock. I will have him stop by your room before he leaves. Where do you want him to take this package? My house?"

"If you don't mind. It may be dangerous. It will be money, a lot of money."

"It will be safe at my house, Senhor."

"I didn't mean that. I meant it may not be safe for you, especially if the Lieutenant should get the idea that you have it."

"No one," he declared, "not even that one, would look in the *favelas* for money. We will take care of it."

"Good. It won't be for long. I'll try to move it sometime tomorrow."

He nodded and drove on. We pulled up in front of the hotel.

"I don't know how things will go tomorrow," I said as I got out. "But you'd better come around nine in the morning. Then we'll see what happens."

"All right, Senhor."

I went in. The hotel was still full of policemen, but they didn't stop me and I didn't see Alvares. When I reached my room, I knocked lightly three times.

She opened the door and I stepped inside. She was in my arms before the door was closed.

"You came early," she said later. "That is wonderful." I went to the closet to take off my jacket. "Anyone phone or come to the door?" I asked.

"No one."

I hung up the jacket, not bothering to conceal the gun, for I knew she must have felt it when she was in my arms. I removed the holster and hung it up. A look in the corner of the closet showed me that nothing had been disturbed. I swung the closet door shut and checked the ice bucket. It was empty.

She was curled up on the bed, watching me as I picked up the phone. I ordered a bucket of ice from room service. Then I loosened my tie and sat down.

"It went well?" she asked.

"I think so." I smiled at her. "I had an offer from a pretty blonde."

"I will scratch her eyes out."

"It won't be necessary. I told her I had a better offer." The waiter came with the ice. I fixed both of us a drink. I began to unwind as I sipped mine. We had a couple more, then I left a call for seven-thirty and called it a day.

The phone rang at seven-thirty and I thanked the operator. I went in the bathroom and had a fast shower. When I came out, Carmelita was awake.

"Good morning," she said sleepily.

"It won't be until we've had breakfast. We're going to have a visitor in a few minutes, and we'll order breakfast after he leaves."

"A visitor?"

"He won't be here long, but you'll have to go into the bathroom while he's here."

She raised her eyebrows, but said nothing.

I hadn't had enough sleep and felt it. I poured myself a small drink and lit a cigarette. In a few minutes there was a light knock on the door. I motioned toward the bathroom. Carmelita made a face at me, but went in and closed the door.

A slender young man stood in the hallway, a bag in his hand. "I am Manuel, Senhor," he said.

"Come in," I said. "Let me have the bag and give me a couple of minutes."

I took the bag and went to the closet. I opened the door next to him so that it would block his view. Then I opened the bag. There were two uniforms in it. I took out one and swiftly put the money on top of the other. I replaced the second uniform, packing it down around the money. I looked at the bag. It appeared merely to be full of clothing. When I lifted it, it was not too heavy. I turned and handed it to Manuel.

"Did anyone see you come here?"

"No, Senhor."

"Try not to let anyone see you leaving. And get this to Alcino as quickly as you can."

He smiled. "He is waiting for me at the employees' entrance."

"Good," I said. "I will give Alcino money for you for last night and this morning."

"Thank you, Senhor."

I opened the door and looked out. There was no one in sight, so I motioned for him to go. I closed the door after him and crossed my fingers.

"All right, Carmelita," I called. "You may come out now."

She came back and climbed into bed. "I am hungry," she announced.

I called room service and ordered breakfast. It came in a very few minutes, and we ate. "Now," I said, when we'd finished coffee, "I want you to get dressed and go home."

"Why?"

"It may get rough around here before long, and I don't want you here if it does."

She got dressed silently and, when she was ready, stood in the center of the room looking at me. "Will I see you again?" she asked quietly.

"I don't know, Carmelita," I said soberly. "I hope so, but I can't be sure. Do you have a phone where you live?"

She smiled. "I wrote it down for you last night. It is on the desk." Then she came into my arms, but only for a minute. "Until we meet again," she said in Portuguese. She opened the door and almost ran out.

The room seemed empty after she was gone. But I had no time to sit and brood on it. I phoned room service and asked them to come and get the breakfast dishes and to bring me a newspaper. Then I got dressed.

The waiter arrived, gave me the newspaper, and wheeled the breakfast cart out.

I took my gun from the holster, unlocked the door, and made myself comfortable on the bed. The gun was in my lap as I read the paper.

It was a little before nine when the knock came. I held the paper with one hand and picked up my gun. "Come in," I called.

The door opened and they came in—Betty Bell and Peter Jackson. As they closed the door, I let the newspaper drop so they could see the gun.

"Relax, friends," I said. "Betty, toss your bag over on the bed—gently."

She did as I told her. I pulled it over with my left hand, opened it, and felt inside. There was a gun there. I lifted it out, holding it by the trigger guard. It was a .38 with a one-inch barrel. I swung my feet to the floor and carried the gun over to the dresser.

"Now, Pete," I said, "turn around and put your hands on the wall above your head."

He did as I told him. I walked over, holding the gun so that I could watch both of them, and ran my left hand over him. He wasn't carrying a gun.

I went back, opened a drawer in the dresser, and nudged Betty's gun into it. I pushed the drawer closed and went back to sit on the bed.

"I imagine," I said, "that you had some idea of coming in, holding a gun on me, and then searching the place. Well, go ahead. You can look freely anywhere except the dresser—and I'll show that to you."

My offer took some of the desire from them, but they went to work while I watched. They were at least very thorough. Finally, they had finished. I walked over to the dresser, keeping enough distance between them and me to be safe, and showed them each drawer.

"Well?" I said.

They both sat down and stared at me. Suddenly the girl started cursing me. She had quite a vocabulary.

"And I thought you were the dainty, feminine type," I said when she ran out of breath. "Now let's get down to the practical facts. Your money is gone. You can't get it back, and the good Lieutenant Alvares can't get his sticky fingers on it either. I realize that it's a great disappointment to all three of you, but that's the way it is."

"When did you grab it?" Jackson asked. His voice was husky and his face pale.

"Right after you went out last night."

"But the cops was all over the joint."

"I know," I said gently. "I saw them frequently."

"Then," the blonde said, "you already had the money when I talked to you last night?"

"Yes."

She started to curse me again, but faltered in mid-stride. She was becoming more aware of the situation.

"That's right," I told her. "It's tight. All you have left is pocket money, and I imagine that isn't much. You can't stay here without money."

"We'll manage," she said.

"You mean Fonesca?" I asked. They both looked surprised. "What did you give him? A hundred thousand dollars for an interest in his club and for not mentioning that Betty was gone—to the ladies' room—long enough last night to have killed Sforza and return? You expect to be able to live on that investment? It'll be nothing. I doubt if Fonesca will do anything about enlarging the club with your money."

"But it's a successful club," Jackson said.

"Sure it is. But Fonesca isn't a successful owner. He likes to gamble, and most of the time he loses. At the moment, his club is mortgaged up to the hilt, and he's in debt for more than that. I doubt if he's going to change. You certainly don't have control of the club, and if anyone takes it away from him, it'll be the people who hold the mortgage. And while we're at it, you might as well face something else. If Alvares ever gets the idea that it was Betty who killed Sforza instead of Pete, Fonesca will fold like whipped cream in a high wind."

They were silent for a minute. "What are you suggesting?" the girl said at last.

"I'm not suggesting anything," I said cheerfully. "But it's obvious that you have only two choices. Neither one is very good, I admit."

"What are they?"

"You can voluntarily return to the United States—with me. There you will face several charges, including murder in the first degree. You will get a fair trial. You might even find a smart lawyer who will try to prove the money I've taken from you is not the same money that was stolen from the armored truck. Or you can stay here and be tried in a Brazilian court for the murder of Joe Sforza. I don't know what sort of trial you'll get, but I imagine that Alvares will be a bit peevish with the money gone."

"I had nothing to do with it," the girl said quickly. "It was Pete."

"Lying bitch," he said. "You killed all of them. It was all your idea."

"You see," I said. "I might point out, however, that there is the gun. I'm sure it was used on Sforza, and probably on the others. I haven't touched anything except the trigger guard. It is probably covered with Betty's fingerprints—and only hers."

"That's right," he said triumphantly.

She was quiet for a minute. "You mean that you'd turn the gun over to the cops here?"

"Of course," I said. "What else could I do?"

She told me. It was not a ladylike expression.

"What if we go back?" Jackson asked.

"Then I'd have to try to get the gun back there."

"I think we ought to go," he said to her. "I don't like cops anywhere, but that Alvares is the worst cop I ever saw. And if he don't get no money, he's going to turn real mean."

She looked at me, her eyes blank. "How much time do we have?"

"Take a couple of hours," I said. "I'll check with you."

"We don't even have enough for plane fare," Jackson said bitterly.

"I'll buy your tickets, if you decide to go," I told him.

She stood up. "Let's get out of here. It smells like a police station."

He followed her from the room.

As soon as they were gone, I buckled on the holster and placed my gun in it. I put on my coat. I considered the other gun for a minute. Then I dropped it into my pocket.

I walked down to the next floor and knocked on Fred Bruce's door. He opened it, and I saw he was just having his breakfast. But he was alone. I stepped inside.

"What's up?" he asked.

"We may be going home today," I said.

"All of us?"

I nodded. "I'll know in a couple of hours. In the meantime, I've got a problem."

"What?"

I pulled the gun from my pocket, holding it by the trigger guard. "This—how to sneak it back into the States without getting caught on this end and also not to destroy the fingerprints on it completely."

"What is it?"

"The gun that killed Sforza. And I think it's the one that killed Myers, Dallin, and Petrie, as well as the two guards."

He grinned. "Give it to me. I'll get it through for you."

I put it down on his dresser. "Glad to get rid of it. Stick around. I'll be in touch with you later."

I went back upstairs and got my sealing wax from the room. Then I took an elevator down. I didn't see any cops around the lobby. I went to a public phone and looked up the American Consul. I stepped into the booth and called the number.

"My name is Milo March," I said when the phone was answered. "I'm an American citizen and I want to speak to the Consul—although I do not know his name."

"It's Mr. Phillips," a girl said. "Just a minute, please."

The minute delivered me to a voice of a male secretary. I repeated what I'd said to the girl. He wanted to know what it was about.

"I work for a large American company," I said, "and it has to do with their interests. I prefer not to go into details, except with the Consul."

"One moment," he said.

It was more like three moments, but finally another voice came on. "This is he American Consul," he said. "What is it?"

"My name is Milo March," I said. "I am an American citizen and I work for Intercontinental Insurance in New York City. Do you know the company?"

"Yes, indeed," he said. "Harkins, the president, is a very good friend of mine. What can I do for you, Mr. March?"

"I'd rather not go into too much detail, sir," I said. "I came down here on behalf of Intercontinental. In the course of carrying out my duties, I have come into possession of some property which belongs to Intercontinental or one of their clients. This property was illegally secured in the United States and brought into Brazil. The return of it will probably be up to the State Department and the courts. In the meantime, however, there is a local official who would like to obtain it for his personal use. I would like to put it in your custody until such time as its return can be determined."

"I see," he said dryly. "I gather that you would rather not tell me the nature of this property?"

"I think it would be wiser, sir."

"How large is it?"

"It consists of one briefcase and one small suitcase. I suggest that I lock both of them and seal the locks with wax, then leave them with you and deliver the keys to New York."

"You seem to have thought of everything," he observed. He was silent for a minute. "I presume you have identification?"

"Yes, sir. But you can also phone Intercontinental collect. I work directly for Martin Raymond, vice-president."

"All right," he said. "How soon will you be here?"

"Within the hour, sir."

I left the phone booth and walked through the lobby. Alcino was waiting out front. So were two police cars. I got into the cab.

"Everything went all right?" I asked.

"Yes," he said. "There was no problem. Where to, Senhor?"

"The first thing is to lose the two cops who are behind us. Can we do it?"

"Leave it to me, Senhor."

It took perhaps twenty minutes of weaving through the city, but we finally ended up on a little street with no one behind us. "Now where, Senhor?" Alcino asked cheerfully.

"I want to stop at a store where I can buy some luggage."

He nodded and turned at the next street. He soon stopped in front of a small store that carried nothing but luggage. I went in and bought a small suitcase. I brought it back to the taxi.

"Now to your house," I said.

Alcino's wife was flustered by our arrival, but she and the children withdrew to the kitchen, and Alcino produced the briefcase and the bag from beneath an old couch. He watched silently while I packed the money in the suitcase, locked it, and covered the lock with sealing wax.

"That is much money, Senhor," he said finally. "It is yours?"

"No. It belongs to the company for which I work."

"It is much money," he repeated.

We carried it out to the taxi, and I told him where I wanted to go. It took us about a half hour. We pulled up in front of a handsome building. I got out with the suitcase and brief-case and went to the door. I gave my name and asked for the Consul. I was immediately shown into his office.

"Mr. March?" he said. "May I see your passport and your other identification?"

I pulled out my wallet and showed my papers to him. He examined them closely and nodded.

"My secretary will give you a receipt for the bags as you go out," he said.

"Thank you," I replied. "I may want to ask one more favor."

"What?"

"I hope to leave for America sometime today. There will be three other American citizens with me. The local official I mentioned might possibly be at the airport and try to put obstacles in our way."

"Who is this official?"

"A Lieutenant Floriano Alvares."

"I have heard of him," the Consul said grimly. "Call me if you think it necessary. I believe I will be here all day."

I thanked him and left. On the way out, the secretary gave me the receipt. I went out to the taxi and told Alcino to take me back to the hotel.

When I got there, I went up to Jackson's room. I could hear voices inside. I knocked, and after a minute the door opened. Their luggage was on the floor in two different groups.

"I see you have decided to return," I said.

"You give us no choice," the blonde said sullenly.

"We checked about Fonesca," Jackson said. "You were right. She was so damn smart she never thought of checking on him. The big brain."

"Shut up," she said.

"I'll get reservations," I told them.

I went downstairs to the reservation desk. "Is there a plane for New York City this afternoon?" I asked.

"Yes, Senhor." The clerk glanced at a clock. "There is one that leaves in one hour and twenty minutes. You wish a reservation?"

"Four reservations," I said.

He looked surprised, but after a brief conversation he told me I could have them. I gave him the four names, paid him, and took the tickets. I phoned Jackson and Fred Bruce and told them what time we were leaving. Then I phoned the Consul and told him. He promised he'd be there.

I checked all four of us out of the hotel and paid the bills. Finally, I went upstairs and packed my own things. A few minutes later, we all assembled in the lobby and went out together. I put Fred and Jackson in one cab and took the blonde with me in Alcino's taxi.

The Consul was already at the airport when we arrived. He stood to one side while we went through the formalities of leaving. We had just finished when Lieutenant Alvares came striding in. He looked as if he were in a rage. His looks didn't improve when he recognized the American Consul.

He strode over to where the four of us stood. "So," he said in Portuguese, "you have decided to leave us?"

The others did not understand him. "Yes," I said. "It has been a nice visit, but there comes a time when one must return home."

"To be sure," he sneered. "Is this all of your possessions?"

"Yes," I said.

"I'm sure that no one will object if I also look through them?"

"Of course not," I said politely. "Please do."

He went over and opened the first bag he came to.

"Hey," Fred said, "what's he doing?"

"He wants to look through our things. It can do no harm."

"I don't want him pawing through my things," the blonde said angrily.

"It could be worse," I reminded her.

He went from bag to bag, getting angrier as he went. Finally, he finished the last one and came back to me. "Where is the money?" he demanded.

"What money?" I asked. "I told you in the beginning that I knew of no money. All the money I have amounts to about twenty-five dollars." That was true. I had given Alcino ten dollars for his cousin's nephew and a hundred dollars for himself, and I was left with twenty-five dollars and some change.

"You know what money I mean, Senhor March," Alvares said intensely. "What have you done with it? It is illegal to remove it from the country."

"I have no money," I repeated. "None of us have any except what is in our pockets. You have already examined our luggage."

He glared at me in frustration, striking the side of his leg with his hand. "I see you are still carrying your gun," he suddenly said.

"Yes."

"If you have canceled your bond, you have no right to carry it."

"But I haven't," I said. "I realize that it means I will forfeit the bond, but I naturally do not want to break any of your laws."

I could see that he was gritting his teeth. "I have sent a request to your New York police for the serial number of your American gun, but I have not yet received a reply. I would prefer that you did not leave until I do."

"Is that a request or a demand, Lieutenant?"

"A request."

"Then I'm afraid that I must refuse. I am needed in New York. If you think there are reasons why I should stay, why not speak to the American Consul, who is standing over there?"

He made a noise deep in his throat and stamped away. After a few steps, he turned to look at me. "I hope we meet again, Senhor March." With that he was gone.

I barely had time to phone Carmelita, and then we were on the plane. A few minutes later it took off. I dozed most of the way back.

When we came down in New York, Fred Bruce was the first one off the plane. As Pete Jackson and Betty Bell stepped out, he arrested them.

I reached Customs ahead of them and was through quickly. I went to a phone and called Martin Raymond.

"It's Milo," I said when I got him. "I'm back. The money is all recovered except for a little over a hundred thousand dollars. I couldn't get it out, but I put it in two bags, locked and sealed them, and turned them over to the American Consul. You'll probably have no trouble getting them."

"Good boy," he said. "What about the criminals?"

"They're all dead but two. They just landed with me and are under arrest. I'll give you a full report in a day or two."

"Good," he said. "I know your expenses ran pretty high, Milo, but I think I can persuade the Board to give you a bonus on this."

"You'd better," I said, and hung up.

As I stepped out of the booth, Fred Bruce went by with his two prisoners. I watched them walking away and thought of the four who hadn't walked away. It reminded me of the ten little Indians.

And like them, this story would not really end until "there were none."

ANNOTATED BIBLIOGRAPHY: BOOKS BY KENDELL FOSTER CROSSEN

In addition to his own full name and "Ken Crossen," Crossen published books under several pseudonyms: M.E. Chaber, Christopher Monig, Richard Foster, Clay Richards, and Bennett Barlay. The books in this list are organized by pseudonym. The editions are all United States publications; most were also published in Canada and the U.K. Many were translated into European languages, including French, Italian, German, Dutch, Swedish, Norwegian, Danish, Czech, Rumanian, and Finnish, as well as Hebrew and Japanese.

As by Kendell Foster Crossen

The Big Dive. Hardcover: E.P. Dutton, 1959. Col. Maj. Kim Locke, U.S. Army intelligence, investigates the disappearance of a Royal Navy frogman who was examining a Russian ship. Locke works with a military working dog (a Hungarian Puli) named Dante. Not in Paperback Library series. See under pen name Clay Richards for another Kim Locke book.

Once Upon a Star: A Novel of the Future. Hardcover: Henry Holt & Co., 1953. Humorous science fiction featuring Manning Draco, an intergalactic insurance investigator.

Four stories reprinted from *Thrilling Wonder Stories* magazine: "The Merakian Miracle," "The Regal Rigelian," "The Polluxian Pretender," and "The Caphian Caper."

Once Upon a Star: The Adventures of Manning Draco, volume 1. Paperback: edited reissue of the 1953 collection, Altus Press, 2013.

The Tortured Path. Hardcover: E.P. Dutton, 1957. Col. Maj. Kim Locke, U.S. Army intelligence, deliberately exposes himself to being brainwashed in Communist China. Paperback: Paperback Library #25, October 1971. See under pen name Clay Richards for another Kim Locke book.

Whistle Stop in Space: The Further Adventures of Manning Draco, volume 2. Paperback: Altus Press, 2013. Humorous science fiction featuring Manning Draco, an intergalactic insurance investigator. Three stories from *Thrilling Wonder Stories* magazine: "Whistle Stop in Space," "Mission to Mizar," and "The Agile Algolian."

Year of Consent. Paperback: Dell, 1954. A dystopian future (1990) that envisions a United States under the tyrannical control of "social engineers" and advertising.

Edited volume: *Adventures in Tomorrow.* Hardcover: Greenberg, 1951. Paperback: Belmont #B75-215, 1968. By Crossen: "Introduction: Houyhnms & Company" and the short story "Restricted Clientele."

Edited volume: *Future Tense.* Hardcover: Greenberg, 1952. By Crossen: "Introduction: Tomorrow Is Here to Stay," "Things of Distinction," as by Kendell Foster Crossen (reprinted from *Startling Stories,* March 1952), and "Love Story," as by Christopher Monig.

As by Ken Crossen

The Case of the Curious Heel. First-edition paperback:
William H. Wise, An Eerie Series Publication, 1942 (name
misspelled "Crosson" on title page). Reprinted in *Baffling
Detective Mysteries,* May 1943, and in paperback, Eerie
Series, 1944. A locked-room mystery.

The Case of the Phantom Fingerprints. Paperback: Vulcan #5,
1945. A locked-room mystery featuring private eyes Jason
Jones and Necessary Smith.

Murder Out of Mind. Paperback: Five Star Mystery #2, Greene
Publishing Co., 1945. Featuring Chariman Fosdick "Fuzzy"
Van Dyke, "celebrated raconteur, wit and radio star," and
playwright Frank Bruce.

Edited volume: *Murder Cavalcade.* Hardcover: Duell,
Sloan & Pearce, 1946. By Crossen: "The Crime in the
Envelope," reprinted from *Banner Mysteries,* March
1945, where the byline was as by Bennett Barlay. This
was the first of the Mystery Writers of America (MWA)
anthologies. Most sources give the editor simply as the
MWA, but both *Twentieth Century Crime & Mystery Writers,* ed. John M. Reilly (Macmillan, 1980, p. 404), and a
historical survey on the MWA website confirm that Ken
Crossen was the editor.

As by M.E. Chaber

See page 2 for a list of Milo March titles.

The Acid Nightmare. Hardcover: Holt, Rinehart & Winston,

1967. Paperback: Paperback Library #64-757, 1972. A young adult novel featuring Johnny Blake, a high school dropout who is introduced to LSD by a syndicate punk. His first trip is groovy, but the second is a nightmare that lands him in jail, accused of murder.

"The Fix." Unpublished manuscript, written c. 1970. In the Kendell Foster Crossen collection at the Howard Gotlieb Archival Research Center, Boston University. A novel for teenagers featuring George Lyman, a young undercover detective who enters the hippie world in Los Angeles to crack an underground drug ring. The book was announced by Holt, Rinehart & Winston for 1971 but never published, owing to a disagreement over the use of slang. The author insisted that he had used accurate Los Angeles youth slang and refused to substitute the New York slang that his editor believed was the correct choice.

As by Christopher Monig

Abra-Cadaver. Hardcover: E.P. Dutton, 1958. Paperbacks: Dell #0007, July 1965; Paperback Library #20, May 1971. Featuring Brian Brett, insurance investigator. This novel was the basis for an episode of the TV series *77 Sunset Strip* (April, 17, 1959).

The Burned Man. Hardcover: E.P. Dutton, 1956. Paperbacks: Dell #992, 1958, as *Don't Count the Corpses;* Paperback Library #21, June 1971. Featuring Brian Brett, insurance investigator.

The Lonely Graves Hardcover: E.P. Dutton, 1960. Paperback:

Paperback Library #23, August 1971. Featuring Brian Brett, insurance investigator.

Once Upon a Crime. Hardcover: E.P. Dutton, 1959. Paperback: Paperback Library #22, July 1971. Featuring Brian Brett, insurance investigator.

As by Richard Foster

Bier for a Chaser. Paperback: Fawcett Gold Medal #899, 1959. Featuring Pete Draco, private detective.

Blonde and Beautiful. Paperback: Popular Library #667, 1955. Featuring Ciro Blake, private detective.

The Girl from Easy Street. Paperback: Popular Library, Eagle # EB32, 1955. Based on the story "Death Bait," as by Kendell Foster Crossen, in *Mobsters: Stories of the Fight against the Underworld,* December 1952.

The Invisible Man Murders. Paperback: Five Star Mystery #5, Greene Publishing Co., 1945. A locked-room mystery featuring Tibetan detective Chin Kwang Kham.

The Laughing Buddha Murders. Paperback: Vulcan #3, 1944, as by Richard Foster. Reprint of a story with the same title, as by Ken Crossen, *Flynn's Detective Fiction,* January 1943. A locked-room mystery featuring Tibetan detective Chin Kwang Kham.

The Rest Must Die. Paperback: Fawcett Gold Medal #853, 1959. A nuclear bomb hits New York City, and the only survivors are those in the underground subway system. Featuring Bob Randall, of the Chaber, Crossen and Monig Advertising Agency.

Too Late for Mourning. Paperback: Fawcett Gold Medal #995, 1960. Featuring private detective Pete Draco.

As by Clay Richards

Death of an Angel. Hardcover: Bobbs-Merrill, 1963. Featuring Grant Kirby, U.S. Postal Inspector. Bomb-by-post murder of a New York City mayoral candidate in the 1890s.

The Gentle Assassin. Hardcover: Bobbs-Merrill, 1964. Lt. Col. Kim Locke, U.S. Army intelligence, goes to Cuba to trace two State Department defectors.

The Marble Jungle. Hardcover: Ivan Obolensky, 1961. Featuring Grant Kirby, U.S. Postal Inspector. Kirby goes undercover as a riverboat gambler in New Orleans to solve a case of mail robbery and murder. Set in the 1890s.

Who Steals My Name. Hardcover: Bobbs-Merrill, 1964. Featuring Blake Morgan, U.S. Postal Inspector, following the paper trail of a forger.

As by Bennett Barlay

Satan Comes Across. Paperback reprint: Eerie #4, 1945. Featuring Larry Donald, playwright and novelist. Reprinted from the serial in *Detective Fiction Weekly,* March 9, 1940; March 16, 1940; and March 23, 1940.

ABOUT THE AUTHOR

Kendell Foster Crossen (1910–1981), the only child of Samuel Richard Crossen and Clo Foster Crossen, was born on a farm outside Albany in Athens County, Ohio—a village of some 550 souls in the year of this birth. His ancestors on his mother's side include the 19th-century songwriter Stephen Collins Foster ("Oh! Susanna"); William Allen, founder of Allentown, Pennsylvania; and Ebenezer Foster, one of the Minute Men who sprang to arms at the Lexington alarm in April 1775.

Ken went to Rio Grande College on a football scholarship but stayed only one year. "When I was fairly young, I developed the disgusting habit of reading," says Milo March, and it seems Ken Crossen, too, preferred self-education. He loved literature and poetry; favorite authors included Christopher Marlowe and Robert Service. He also enjoyed participant sports and was a semi-pro fighter in the heavyweight class. He became a practicing magician and had a passion for chess.

After college Ken wrote several one-act plays that were produced in a small Cleveland theater. He worked in steel mills and Fisher Body plants. Then he was employed as an insurance investigator, or "claims adjuster," in Cleveland. But he left the job and returned to the theater, now as a performer: a tumbling clown in the Tom Mix Circus; a comic and carnival barker for a tent show, and an actor in a medicine show.

In 1935, Ken hitchhiked to New York City with a typewriter under his arm, and found work with the WPA Writers' Project, covering cricket for the *New York City Guidebook*. In 1936, he was hired by the Munsey Publishing Company as associate editor of the popular *Detective Fiction Weekly*. The company asked him to come up with a character to compete with The Shadow, and thus was born a unique superhero of pulps, comic books, and radio—The Green Lama, an American mystic trained in Tibetan Buddhism.

Crossen sold his first story, "The Aaron Burr Murder Case," to *Detective Fiction Weekly* in September 1939, but says he didn't begin to make a living from writing till 1941. He tried his hand at publishing true crime magazines, comics, and a picture magazine, without great success, so he set out for Hollywood. From his typewriter flowed hundreds of stories, short novels for magazines, scripts radio, television, and film, nonfiction articles. He delved into science fiction in the 1950s, starting with "Restricted Clientele" (February 1951). His dystopian novels *Year of Consent* and *The Rest Must Die* also appeared in this decade.

In the course of his career Ken Crossen acquired six pseudonyms: Richard Foster, Bennett Barlay, Kent Richards, Clay Richards, Christopher Monig, and M.E. Chaber. The variety was necessary because different publishers wanted to reserve specific bylines for their own publications. Ken based "M.E. Chaber" on the Hebrew word for "author," *mechaber.*

In the early '50s, as M.E. Chaber, Crossen began to write a series of full-length mystery/espionage novels featuring Milo March, an insurance investigator. The first, *Hangman's Harvest,* was published in 1952. In all, there are twenty-two Milo March novels. One, *The Man Inside,* was made into a British film starring Jack Palance.

Most of Ken's characters were private detectives, and Milo was the most popular. Paperback Library reissued twenty-five Crossen titles in 1970–1971, with covers by Robert McGinnis. Twenty were Milo March novels, four featured an insurance investigator named Brian Brett, and one was about CIA agent Kim Locke.

Crossen excelled at producing well-plotted entertainment with fast-moving action. His research skills were a strong asset, back when research meant long hours searching library microfilms and poring over street maps and hotel floorplans. His imagination took him to many international hot spots, although he himself never traveled abroad. Like Milo March, he hated flying ("When you've seen one cloud, you've seen them all").

Ken Crossen was married four times. With his first wife he had three children (Stephen, Karen, Kendra) and with his second a son (David). He lived in New York, Florida, Southern California, Nevada, and other parts of the country. Milo March moves from Denver to New York City after five books of the series, with an apartment on Perry Street in Greenwich Village; that's where Ken lived, too. His and Milo's favorite watering hole was the Blue Mill Tavern, a short walk from the apartment.

Ken Crossen was a combination of many of the traits of his different male characters: tough, adventuresome, with a taste for gin and shapely women. But perhaps the best observation was made in an obituary written by sci-fi writer Avram Davidson, who described Ken as a fundamentally gentle person who had been buffeted by many winds.